DOMINION

DOMINION

A NOVEL

ADDIE E. CITCHENS

FARRAR, STRAUS AND GIROUX

NEW YORK

Farrar, Straus and Giroux
120 Broadway, New York 10271

EU Representative: Macmillan Publishers Ireland Ltd, 1st Floor, The Liffey
Trust Centre, 117–126 Sheriff Street Upper, Dublin 1, DO1 YC43

Title-page art by Blojfo / Shutterstock.com.

Library of Congress Cataloging-in-Publication Data
Names: Citchens, Addie E., 1980– author.
Title: Dominion : a novel / Addie E. Citchens.
Description: First edition. | New York : Farrar, Straus and Giroux, 2025.
Identifiers: LCCN 2025003342 | ISBN 9780374609337 (hardcover)
Subjects: LCGFT: Novels.
Classification: LCC PS3603.I88 D66 2025 | DDC 813/.6—dc23/
    eng/20250321
LC record available at https://lccn.loc.gov/2025003342

Designed by Gretchen Achilles

Our books may be purchased in bulk for specialty retail/wholesale, literacy,
corporate/premium, educational, and subscription box use. Please contact
MacmillanSpecialMarkets@macmillan.com.

www.fsgbooks.com
Follow us on social media at @fsgbooks

10 9 8 7 6 5 4 3 2 1

For my Marys:
Granny Mary, with little formal education,
you taught me everything. I write because of your
razor-edged word and intelligence.
Auntie Mary, I miss you every day, and I fashion you
in every bad-mother-shut-your-mouth I write.
You were the prototype.

DOMINION

THE STORY OF
THE SEVEN SEALS

as commissioned by The SEVEN SEALS Anniversary Committee,
compiled by First Lady Priscilla A. Stringer Winfrey, 1995

The Seven Seals M. B. Church was organized in June 1930 and a building erected at 1430 H. H. Milne Boulevard, in Dominion, two city blocks from its eventual home at 1600 H. H. Milne Boulevard. The founding members, Rev. Perry McMillian, Sis. Amelia Reinhart, Bro. Marvel Twine, Sis. Harriet Lindsey, Bro. Isaiah Lindsey, Bro. Bethel Green, and Dr. and Mrs. Herbert Lampkin, came together from their former institution in pursuit of decency and the execution of God's order. In its sixty-five years of operation, Seven Seals has had just four leaders. Perry McMillian served as the Seals' first shepherd until his retirement in 1947. Rev. Frederick Jones served until his death in 1959. Rev. Beauty Watkins was installed in January 1960 and served until his retirement in 1976. In 1976, Rev. Sabre J. Winfrey, Jr., was installed as leader of the congregation. Under his guidance, the Seals' membership has increased tenfold, and an era of holy prosperity has arisen.

CHURCH MILESTONES

June 1930   First Sabbath Service: "Where Two or Three Are Gathered."

February 1931   Cornerstone laid on 1430 H. H. Milne location.

April 1932   First sermon preached inside 1430 H. H. Milne.

January 1933   Trustees and elders voted to add additional Sunday of worship, with services to be held on both the second and fourth Sundays of each month.

November 1940   First delegation sent to the Gathering of the Saints in Memphis.

June 1954   Sis. Ophelia Murphy donated fifty folding chairs and five tables as a faith offering to the commission to build a fellowship hall for the Seals.

January 1955   Seven Seals purchased a baptismal pool to be installed beneath the choir stand. Heretofore, baptisms had been performed in Dundee Creek in nearby Dundee, Mississippi.

December 1958   The first annual Christmas musical, held at H. H. Milne Fellowship Hall. This spectacle has since grown into a three-night performance that includes beautiful, historically accurate costumery, original music, live animals, and a drive-through manger scene.

April 1963   The first annual Easter musical held at the fellowship hall. The Easter musical has since grown into three nights of performance that include beautiful, historically accurate costumery, original music, and a heart-wrenching crucifixion scene that underscores Christ's ultimate sacrifice.

February 1965   The Seven Seals hosted the Reverend Dr. Martin Luther King, Jr., on Valentine's Sunday.

March 1966   Services expanded to include all Sundays of the month except the fifth.

July 1970   Seven Seals for Africa delegation travels for missionary work in Kenya and Nigeria.

June 1971   First Saints vs. Sinners Fundraising Banquet (for school supplies for the community).

April 1972   To accommodate the growing population of saints, the Seven Seals Building Fund was kicked off. Luster and Associates was commissioned to design the building.

July 1972   First annual Vacation Bible School, as directed by Sis. Lily Washington. First Lady Mabel Watkins and Sis. Brenda-Gale Malone started the youth choir.

May 1975   The church instituted its transportation ministry, led by Bro. Billy Taylor.

January 1976   Rev. Sabre Winfrey, Jr., installed as pastor. Rev. Winfrey's tutelage gave rise to the Boys to Men Ministry (assisted by

Rev. Vernon Saffold), the annual Seven Seals Rally, and the Youth Raising Our Voices (YROV) benefit concert, featuring choirs from the tristate region.

January 1978 Groundbreaking ceremony held for the new church building. A bus was purchased for the transportation ministry.

March 1980 Rev. Sabre Winfrey, Jr., led the march from 1430 to 1600 H. H. Milne in celebration of the new building as well as the fiftieth church anniversary. The theme was "To Boldly Go." With a seating capacity of one thousand, the Seven Seals' new home boasted a ballroom for weddings, repasts, and other holy events, eight classrooms, a pastor's study, a music studio, and a counseling room. The church also purchased property along Lemon Street to renovate as low-income housing for the community.

August 1982 The Seven Seals Day Care opened its doors to provide Christ-centered childcare and family support for children aged infant to four years.

October 1982 Seven Seals for the Hungry and Poor Saints opened the Manna Soul Food Restaurant. Its mission was twofold: to provide nutritious, delicious Delta delicacies and to provide meaningful work opportunity for the indigent and poor.

August 1990 Rev. Sabre Winfrey, Jr., and the Seven Seals, in conjunction with Andy Luckett, Esq., and the Carnegie Mellon Foundation, launched "And Bid Them Sing," a multiple-city civil rights / blues history tour.

January 1991 Bishop G. E. Patterson blessed the renovation. The Heaven-Bound Soldiers led the march to consecrate the new light fixtures in the ballroom, the outdoor spotlighting, the PA system, and the new electronic marquee.

January 1992 The first computer was purchased, and the Seals began to computerize its records.

February 1994 State-of-the-art multiple media system installed in the church sanctuary recording studio.

Of special note: The Seven Seals owes its prosperity to the will of God and the help of several long-serving saints. Church treasurers: Bro.

Isaiah Lindsey (1930–1976) and Bro. Whittie Johnson (1976–present). Church secretaries: Sis. Annie Ford (1930–1960), Sis. Ophelia Murphy (1961–1979), and Sis. Linda Dunlap (1979–present). Sis. Nellie Ford, President of Pastor's Aid Club, 1963–present. Bro. Randy McMillian, church maintenance, 1968–present. Sis. Brenda-Gale Malone, Youth Choir Director, 1972–present.

PROLOGUE

Reverend Sabre Winfrey, Jr., believed without a shadow of a doubt that an idle mind was the devil's workshop, but an idle hand belonged on a behind. A tall, blue-black strap of a man, on Sundays he ministered to the flock of the Seven Seals Missionary Baptist Church, the largest congregation in Dominion and arguably the entire Mississippi Delta, Black or otherwise. He owned WDOZ (easy listening during the week, *The Catfish Fry* on Saturdays, and *Joyful Noise* all day Sunday) and Sabre Cuts Old-Fashioned Barbershop, the only place in town a man could still get a warm shave. There, he sang lead tenor in the quartet; in the mid-eighties, he perfected the Sabre, a razor-edged fade that left just enough hair on top to display the wave pattern. He owned houses on every street in the White House neighborhood but Lincoln and had coached the Dominion Rebels to the 5A state football championships in '90, '92, and '96.

His first lady was Priscilla Stringer of Clarksdale's Zion Funeral Home Stringers. She had a degree in music education from Tougaloo College and could have been Miss America had it not been for her woebegone limp. The women praised her faded-gray eyes, moist, peachy skin, the heavy waves of dull red hair, but they called her Hunchback when she wasn't around—even though she had no hunched back, just a bad hip from when she was five years old and playing funeral with her brothers and sisters. They had laid her into a box their granddaddy had built for selling pecans and hoisted her up, up until she was dizzy with excitement at being so far from the ground. The feeling, though, was fleeting. The box was rotted; she'd come smashing through the bottom, landing heavy on her right side. She remembered the house call from Dr. Levy, too, where he'd poked at her hip once or twice with his thick hairy fingers, pronounced it not broken, and promptly left. In the middle of the night, all these years later, if she lay on it wrong and her pain pills had worn off or Rev had confiscated them, her body would recall the searing pain of that day as well as the scratch of a rock on her cheek or the sharp smell of grass, and always the thud as she landed, but never the miracle of the flight that had come before.

Sabre and Priscilla had five boys: Trey and Moshe (twins), Mack, Ivy, and Emanuel, called Manny, or Wonderboy. The first four looked like more of Sabre's genes had gone into their making, but Wonderboy looked like the best of both of them, and for that Priscilla was glad. For four nauseous years of her life, she had carried these loads on a small frame and a bad hip, and only the last time did she come out with something bearing the imprint of her distortion.

1

I'm just a nobody trying to tell everybody about somebody who can save anybody.

Sabre J. Winfrey

June 4, 2000

MORNING MESSAGE: We're Not Worthy

SCRIPTURAL BACKGROUND: "And I saw in the right hand of Him who sat on the throne, a scroll written inside and on the back, sealed with seven seals. Then I saw a strong angel proclaiming with a loud voice, 'Who is worthy to open the scroll and to loose its seals?' And no one in heaven or on the earth or under the earth was able to open the scroll, or to look at it." Revelation 5:1-3 NKJV

SABRE POINTS: What does the inability of anyone to open the book of judgment tell us about the Christian in the time of John?_____

We know that sin was passed to us through our brother Adam, and we know only the Lamb has walked the earth without sin. Why is John so distraught that none other is worthy to open the book of judgment? How are his views reflective of the Heavenly Father's?_____

_____

Revelation proselytizes the end of history as we know it. How can that acknowledgment make us stronger in our day-to-day walk?_____

The wages of sin is_____,
but the gift of God is_____.

9

PRISCILLA

The duration of Sunday devotional depended on whether or not the Holy Spirit drove Rev into falsetto. As he walked from behind the pulpit to stand between the enormous sprays of magnolia on either side of the altar, I could tell he was headed there.

"Whoooooooooo is?" he croaked down deep and then slid an octave up. "Whoooooooooo is? Who is worthy?"

Rev favored a low bass in his arrangements for contrast and fiddled with every aspect of musicianship. Of course, the sanctuary had been constructed for acoustic excellence. The altar, bandstand, and pulpit lay in the valley with the pews rising on an incline, so that his honey voice floated up to make me shiver. Witnessing him in his element dampened my twenty-five years of fury at Melvistine Evan's beastly self for encouraging me to sit down out of the sanctuary choir when she complained I couldn't get the precision rock right because of my limp. Anyway, Rev sang the first two lines, and Melvistine's hungry eyes were edifying him, and I thought proudly (despite our problems), *That's my man.*

In the early days before the computer, I typed all of the church's programs using a big blue typewriter he let me pick out. I enjoyed key clacking and ink smudges, the tidy paper begging to be used, the busy hum of the machine. I would close the study door and let him tend to the boys, except for whomever was nursing. It made me feel important, even though the sermons I produced based on his notes would end up being used as guideposts or maybe not at all, depending on how the Spirit moved him. I was so proud, proud to be his wife and the mother of his children. Then, I thought we were in this thing together; it took a long while and a harsh fall to see it had never been about *us*, but about him. And even after realizing why he had hired Linda to be his secretary when she couldn't type, spell, or figure her way out of a paper bag, I continued to research and create these programs for him, for the Seals.

But I digress. I was rocking just fine from my seat, and certainly, everyone could hear my beautiful operatic soprano and the precision of my tambourine, loudest when Melvistine called herself leading a song. Besides, sitting down, I looked better than every sister in here, even Katherine, or Kathareen as everybody said, who was barely thirty but recently widowed when her husband was mangled in an accident with an 18-wheeler. Brown and juicy, Kathareen still had all her teeth, had come up on a little money with the wrongful-death settlement, and always had a foot of somebody else's hair affixed to her head. Plus, Deacon Golliday always had to tip over with a pillowcase to cover the big, shiny legs she never saw fit to throw a pair of stockings on.

"Lawd, I got to know: Whoooooooooo is? Who is worthy?" called Rev. "To open up the book of the seven seals?" crooned the quartet in response.

Manny's bass grooved, and Ivy slammed the drums like a maniac. I don't know how many times I had to tell my boys that this was a house of the Lord and not the VFW Lounge. Manny was throwing eyes at somebody; I craned my head to try to follow the direction of his gaze. Church was packed, but in the general vicinity was Kathareen; Maggie's girl, Diamond (it's a shame that somebody saw fit to give that child a stripper's name); and Mary Kay's oldest daughter, the one with the liver lips. I had heard so many things about what that child did with them lips. Merciful father, say it aint that one. Manny was special, my baby—I couldn't bear to have him turned out by some worldly hussy. I twisted a little further for a better look. Did I need to go over there to check the situation out? Rev would be damn inquisitive if I moved, and also too if I got up and walked over there, I would no longer be the best-looking woman in the room. My hip throbbed as if to underscore that point.

I flipped my hand to motion for Bertha Benny. Her brother had the Gulf War syndrome, and he sold his various pain and nerve pills to get crack; she usually had something on hand. She was ushering that Sunday, so by the first offering, she had slipped me a few nerve pills in a yellow handkerchief. I dipped my head low into my gilded Bible and dropped one under my tongue, where it quickly dissolved to dust and bitter. You got the fulfillment quicker thataway. I started to pray. If God didn't protect my baby from ruthless women, who could?

DIAMOND

Where normally I had been a back-row believer, since I began loving Wonderboy, I became a third-row Christian. I had to be able to lay eyes on him quickly if I needed to, felt the rising panic in my chest when I couldn't. Now, he was playing bass, which I think was his favorite, but not his only, or even his best, instrument. He picked up the piano by ear at Seven Seals, before his mama had the chance to teach him at home. Next came the drums and the diddley bow with his uncle, and then there was the guitar that he made wail in the middle of revival, so deep was he in the Spirit. In the third grade, they bussed him to Booker T. Washington Junior High, where he learned the trumpet. For a moment, he eyed the saxophone, but his daddy said a man never oughta put nothing in his mouth but food. He focused his talents on the piano and the guitar; he mainly played Velvet (one of two given to his daddy by Ike Turner) or Sarah, a little acoustic that had belonged to his grandaddy. Although all of the Winfrey boys could sing like angels, if anyone could truly sing his ass off, Wonder wouldn't have nothing to sit on. During one of the Black History Month assemblies at school, the drama teacher played a recording of some Zulu singers, who sounded less like they were singing than vibrating together. Several kids were inexplicably crying. Wonder's voice was like that. It made people feel like crying in a good way.

The summer before sixth grade, he transformed. His voice squeaked, hair shot out like quills around his jaw, and tight, animal thighs began to stress his school khakis out. His face angled up, and he had brooding eyes—even when he was smiling. It was then that they discovered he could run, too, like, really run, and so his daddy had him training with his brothers and the other high school boys in the mornings and afternoons. Each Thursday, the driftwoody bleachers were full of people watching him look like a man among kids. And even when he was playing both sides of the ball on Friday nights at Dominion

High School, and the other boys had more or less caught up to him, he was the only one that got to wear red cleats. He darted through the line like a beast and a dancer. People bought fewer concessions when he was on the field because they didn't want to miss what he would do next.

If he didn't have a big dick, somebody should have stoned him, but everybody knew all the Winfreys did. When he passed, the teachers got nervous; the girls sighed. When he picked you, you didn't giggle about him with your girlfriends, or they would get too jealous and try to slander your name. Me and my siblings were smelly poor when we were younger, and on top of that, my mama went and left, or died, which was shameful in itself. Kids like me usually went through school either being very violent or very quiet. I wasn't a fighter, so I had long ago chosen the latter. In our shared spaces, I was content to watch him, knowing I would never get the chance to love him.

Junior year, I started letting my hair hang wild every day because I heard he liked that. They started saying I must be mixed with something, but who knew? I certainly didn't. It must have worked because one day last September, he was behind me in chemistry and complained to the teacher that he could not see around my hair. It got the class to cracking up and my face burning red. After the bell had rung, as we were leaving, he overtook me.

"Diamond Bailey," he said, like he had just remembered me from somewhere.

My heart sang, but he went on his way down the hall without saying another word. The next day at lunchtime, he upped and asked me to give him what was on my tray, and I did. It was a thing the boys did sometimes if they liked you. The next day we had chili and rice, and he asked me again, and I gave it to him again. He took everything but the fruit cocktail, and I sat with my friend Bunny and side-eyed him, scooping the sap-thin fruit cocktail juice from its molded compartment as my stomach complained. The day after that was Friday, and we were having catfish. You could smell it all up and down the hall.

The catfish came hard-fried on a cloud of white bread, and even though that starchy bread would be stuck to the roof of my mouth for the rest of the day, I spent the morning periods daydreaming about drowning my fish in hot sauce and ketchup and making a sandwich. Well, he was waiting for me in the cafeteria, and I had to tell him no. He laughed, and the other athletes laughed with him. He let me off the hook, but he made sure I saw him taking Shanice's fish from her tray.

The same afternoon, he cornered me in the hall and asked me for my phone number.

That was ten months ago, and now he was my everything, and I was his. He gave me money, and he didn't bother me about no coochie, even though I wanted to give him some, and he would have been justified in asking because he was who he was. But I wasn't a pretend virgin. I was 100 percent a virgin, and it was amazing to him, and me, too, that a girl like me got to be seventeen without even being finger fucked—by a friend of the family or spare uncle at the very least. For that reason, we decided together to save ourselves for each other when the time was right.

Not everybody was in love with Wonderboy, though. A lot of people assumed he thought he was too much, and I could believe that he did. When we were thirteen in Vacation Bible School, Lissandra Betts asked if Jesus had a last name. Lissandra wore Coke bottle glasses and was in special education. Her and all the Bettses were so big and tall you could tell they had plow-hand or blacksmith in their lineage. Nobody made fun of her, though, because her brother, Beefsteak, was colossal and smart as a whip, but he would bang heads over Lissandra. If it had been anybody else, Mother Butler would have thought they were playing with the Lord, but everybody knew Lissandra was sincere. Somebody yelled out, "Of Nazareth." Another somebody said, "Christ," and almost said, "Duh," after that, but they checked themself before Beefsteak could.

"Jesus Winfrey," yelled Wonderboy. "You didn't know? His name was Jesus Winfrey. *Jesus Winfrey, Emanuel Winfrey,* can't yall see?"

Everybody laughed or booed. At other times, he had said his brothers had tried to throw him down a well, or that he had just come from crushing Philistines, or that he had merely one seal left to break, but this time, Mother Butler really got mad. She walked him straight to the pastor's study and stayed gone a long time. He came back smiling.

"What your daddy say?" I overheard one of the boys ask when we were leaving to go home.

"Amen." Wonderboy laughed.

PRISCILLA

The last thing I did after every cleaning was dust my kids' baby pictures. Rev used to ask me why I bothered with those pictures all the time, assuming it was some sort of female sentimentality, but I'd given up cells, blood, life, and careers for them; I couldn't help but need to feel pride. And to be honest, that was the best time of motherhood, when they belonged totally to me, when they couldn't talk and only I could soothe them. That said, I was not one of those women who thought my children's shit didn't stink, but people had to admit that I had some good boys. Trey and Moshe were twenty-four and had a full ride to Meharry; Mack was twenty-two and driving trucks. My knee baby, Ivy, was twenty and studying music over at Ole Miss, and Manny was going into his senior year, set to be salutatorian—all with no children out of wedlock, thank you, Jesus.

I could scarcely believe I had adult kids and that I was this old. I mean I had watched it coming, but still I felt blindsided. Blessedly, my life hadn't happened across my face. Not only did my classmates have multiple grandbabies, their formerly snatched waists lapped over their waistbands, and their mouths had been permanently splintered from years spent drawn around cigarettes. To keep my shape, I pushed back from the table and wore a corset and a pantie girdle every day. I also did calisthenics and rode my bike, and with Rev being so into physical fitness, he approved. Wednesday, I had taken so long cleaning and pattering around the house, it was already mid-afternoon when I decided to take a quick ride. The early June heat had yet to become unbearable; I figured I'd be home in good time to get dinner started.

In minutes, I was pumping down the street on the bike, and soon I cleared the neighborhood. The headiness I got when riding made me feel powerful, strong, and young, all the ways I never felt on my own two feet. I stood up on the pedals and urged the bike into a devilish speed, blazing through downtown via the Red Panther River trail. The river snaked on into the next county, but the trail stopped near the highway. There I dismounted, pushed my bike up the ramp, and paused at the two lanes of road between me and Carpenter's Junk Store. They put their new shipments out on Wednesdays, and I came almost every week to poke around and chat with the clerk, Wilma. Every third word of Wilma's was a curse, but she kept me laughing. It was usually easier for me to have a conversation with folk who weren't in the church—because Barbara, Brenda-Gale, Melvistine, all of them, were too snooty and fake for their own good. Wilma was real. While we were sharing a laugh, Craig Carpenter came around the building.

"You oughta let me throw that bike on the back of my truck and drop you off at home," he told me.

He had a beard and a mouth full of Skoal, but he wasn't bad looking at all, sort of resembled Little Joe from *Bonanza*. I envisioned myself naked beneath him, tickled by a mat of rusty chest hair, squirming under the sweet stench of tobacco in a bed of hay.

"No, thank you," I said.

Rev would have a hissy fit if he found out I was in the car with another man, a white one at that. If a Black woman was in the car with a white man, she was either tricking or cleaning, and Rev wanted his wife associated with neither. I wheeled my bike to the edge of the road, faced a dazzling, sinking sun. A car whooshed by, forcing a reckless shiver up my spine, a feeling so icy and familiar and choke-deep that it took all my might not to fling myself into traffic to see if I could get airborne. I glanced back, and Wilma and Carpenter were there, as if they were making sure I didn't.

I turned the block and was relieved to see Rev's car absent from the driveway; I figured he was probably out somewhere harmonizing. Manny's truck wasn't there either, and I wondered where he might be. If you asked me, he had too much freedom, but I couldn't tell Rev nothing about none of these boys. His trust-them-until-they-proved-you-wrong approach to parenting always frightened me, and I'm certain he wouldn't have been that way if we had daughters. I pushed my bike into the side door, leaned it across from the washer and dryer, and entered the kitchen. The lights were on, but the house seemed unnaturally quiet. After all these years of raising boys, I had yearned for silence. Now, with only one left, quiet proved to be just another thing I thought I'd wanted.

As I washed my hands at the sink in the half bath, I pushed the shade aside and saw Manny's truck in the alley. I had repeatedly warned them against parking there, but they wouldn't be satisfied until a robberman held a gun to their head and stripped them of all their belongings and dignity. I proceeded up the stairs, was poised to knock on his bedroom door, when I heard breathing: hushed and impatient. I gave the door the slightest shove and was looking at Manny from behind, hunched over whatever he was doing. His skin was taut with strength; his rump came right off his back like his father's. A step to the right revealed Maggie's girl on the floor beneath him. Her nipples looked like Cocoa Puffs, and I knew she couldn't have good sense because she shielded them and not her privates. Manny turned his great, boxy head around, and the way he looked me straight in the eye in the midst of this trifling act instantly and thoroughly convinced me that deep down inside there was something wrong with him. I closed my mouth and the door. This was my fault; my mama used to say that if you went looking for trouble, you wouldn't have to go far to find it.

There were harsh whispers behind me, the shrieking of the embarrassed girl. My earlier fulfillment had done a Houdini, and my hip throbbed. I took two pain pills with a nip of the Jack that I kept in an economy-sized box of women's supplies in my closet. When I heard Manny's truck pull out of the alley, I took a bath, and afterwards, I thought over my options from my bedroom. One thing was for sure: I definitely wasn't in the mood to stand in a hot kitchen and cook and then clean up after. While I was contemplating where to call in for takeout, he began knocking on the door, which I ignored. I decided to phone in an order to Borgononi's. By the time the doorbell rang for the delivery, the house had come alive. Manny was playing his guitar, and Rev was holding a lively conversation with somebody in his study. I paid and tipped the guy, but, abandoned by my appetite, left the bags on the kitchen counter.

I peeked in the study to tell Rev the food was there, and then I paused and exhaled, grateful my fulfillment was kicking in. Finally, I went to the door of Manny's room, left open on purpose, I knew. He looked up at me as I was trying to look away; our gaze held a few seconds past ordinary. I broke the stare first, directing it at my bedroom, where I was already lying down in my mind.

"Go eat, son," I said.

DIAMOND

The Winfreys lived up on Ashton Court, the grandest street on Coon Hill, with all the rest of the fancy Black folk. It was proper from the outside, so proper I didn't want to go in, especially not *sneak* in there. But I really would do just about anything for him, so I followed him through a maze of lemon oil and leather. The wood floors shone. Gold and silver tassels hung off everything. A grand piano, huge and stern, sat in the living room. I would love to hear him play it, but he was acting like he was in such a big rush. Above the piano was a portrait of the Winfreys and their boys, all handsome and coordinated in navy and red. If a house could judge, this one would; walking through the perfect rooms made me feel small but heavy and conspicuous, like a bowling ball.

His bedroom was the first at the top of the stairs. He had a red plaid bedspread and trophies on every flat space. I wanted to examine them, but he was dragging his feet out of his shoes and motioning for me to get undressed. His pants dropped with a jingle. His shirt and undershirt sounded softer, a plop. The other times, we did this in my house when Mama was sitting, but he insisted on here for some reason this time. I got naked, lay on the floor, and spread my hair around my shoulders. He sucked on my lips, causing a hungry little sound to come out of me, but before I could really enjoy anything, he was standing, stroking himself. I liked how he sounded when he did this thing, liked how he looked when he tossed his head back and showed the ropes in his neck. Loved how the muscles in his stomach and chest twitched and clenched.

What would the First Lady think at what we were doing? As I smiled slyly to myself, she came into the room behind Wonder, and her mouth fell open. *Ohjesusohgodohjesusohgod!* I couldn't believe she was in the room, especially since I had just been thinking about her. *Ohjesusohgodohjesusohgod!* I had called her up. I knew I had. I brought my arms up to cover my chest. Wonder turned around to her and then around to me and around to her again, but she was gone. I scrambled to my feet and yanked my clothes on over his mess, followed him downstairs, crying the whole time. The First Lady had disappeared into one of the rooms. What was she thinking? I bet she was yakking to all the church ladies right now. I couldn't stop shaking even though it was warm outside. Wonderboy put me into the car, where I cried more.

"Calm down, Diamond. It's OK. It's OK," he said.

"It's not OK! FUCK!"

It was the first time I'd ever cursed at him. He took my hands to still them but was unsuccessful. He gave up, started the truck.

"You hungry?"

Mortified, plus icky with his stuff, I shook my head, and afterwards, there wasn't much more to say. He drove me straight home and walked me to the door, waiting with me as I fumbled with the keys. He tucked some bills in my pocket and brushed my temple with his lips as I was moving away from him. I didn't want to be touched, but I wanted to be hugged, if that made any sense, though I mentioned none of that to him. I slammed myself inside the empty house and let out a long, frustrated scream. At least Maggie was with one of her clients, so I didn't have to worry about her asking what was wrong or coming in no time soon. I just wanted to bathe and get in bed and act like this never happened.

I ran the water very hot and very high and sank down so only my knees and my shoulders stood up. The expression that woman had when she looked down at me had said it all. And then what did my dumb ass do? I covered my titties. I made up my mind to call the First Lady after my bath and say, "For your information I'm a virgin. I was just doing that to stay that way, so don't judge me, bitch." But then I decided against it. This embarrassment felt karmic. I wondered if she remembered me from way back. One year, my birth mama had wrangled me and my older sister, Cricket, up to go to Finer Woman-hood Week in the Eliza P. Walker school auditorium. It was a program sponsored by the First Lady's sorority, and they taught girls about pads and cramps, how to sit with our ankles crossed, what to wear to keep our bodies from moving under our clothes. Me and Cricket ate like wolves at the reception table every day.

"My, you girls are hungry," the First Lady said in her chirpy voice.

I didn't get the sense that she was purposely making fun

23

of us, but the bitch had to have known we were hungry. The chocolate cupcake I was eating, which had previously been moist and delicious, went sour. I crumbled the remainder of it in my hand, while Cricket kept eating and looking at the First Lady stupid. To my dismay, Cricket took the moment to begin hobbling and mimicking the woman's walk. I was smirking at first, but then I felt bad.

"Cricket, stop!"

But she kept on until the First Lady's face dropped, and she scurried off the other way. Something told me she left to go cry. Her hollowed expression was burned into my mind, reminding me so much of the shock she had when she walked in on us. I heaved myself out of the tub, half-heartedly swiped my toothbrush across my teeth, put on a nightgown, jumped in bed, and yanked the covers over my head. What would Maggie think of me when the First Lady told her what happened?

I couldn't remember if my real ma ever broached the topic of the birds and bees with me and my siblings. I didn't remember many of her words period, but I remember her habits clearly, like how she would wash a dish ten times or scrub a long-gone stain until something in her mind clicked, and she could leave it alone. She last worked at the Soap Opera Laundromat, and I had a begrudging pride for the work she did—starkly uniform T-shirts; elegant, precise towels; even the sheets she folded looked like they came right out of the pack. It wasn't unusual for her to work over, finishing orders well after she was supposed to get off. The last time me and Cricket went up there, the Soap part of the sign was dead, but Opera shone neon green. Inside was simultaneously bright and shadowy like a spaceship, and somebody's tennis shoes were having a row in one of the dryers. Way at the tables in the rear, Mama was folding and refolding a man's dress shirt, frustrated by a stubborn shoulder. The white patch of hair at the front of her head made her look tired, much older than her thirty-two years.

"Sometimes, shit don't be right no matter how hard you try," she wept.

Since I was little, I had some habits, too. Most times, I added up the letters in the words people said to me. Somewhere along the way, I concluded that the closer the number came to ten, the more likely it was that the person was telling the truth. Letter counting was a useful tool for me, but I didn't tell anybody about it because maybe it made me crazy like her.

PRISCILLA

On the evening of February 14, 1976, my husband explained to me that because Eve ate the apple, I would have to "eat the snake." The act shocked and appalled me, but I was submissive to my husband like I thought I was supposed to be. The next day was a Sunday; I couldn't believe he stood up in the pulpit and preached all the same. It became a habit of his that while he watched the old bang-bang shoot-'em-up Westerns on the TV in the study, he regularly sawed into my mouth, and I tried my best to protect the back of my throat when he got too zealous. I knew in the scheme of things, this probably wasn't so bad a thing to do, especially since this was my husband, but try as I could, I could not get comfortable with it. It got so that I had to tell somebody. I don't know what I was to her, but Bertha Benny was my best friend, the one I told my secrets to. Of course, she didn't take me seriously.

"Well, I guess something must be wrong with Betty Jean's jaws," she said, laughing. "Because she was everybody go-to."

"I'm not playing, Bertha. Tell me what to do."

"Well, personally, I don't mind it, but if you really do, the more you act like you like it, the quicker it'll be over with."

And so the next time, I gathered all the moisture I could in my mouth and wiggled my head back and forth. I looked him straight in the eye, and he looked me straight in the eye, and it didn't take long until he was glugging out into my mouth. And then his hand came twice so disrespectfully across the back of my head. He held my chin and eyed me suspiciously.

"Where did you learn that at?" he spat. "Huh? Who you been hanging around?"

Who had Manny been hanging around? Where had he learned that thing? What did that say about him? Was it somehow connected to Rev's depraved behaviors? I thought, with horror, of what any of my boys might be doing with women. My mind found that silly girl, clutching her breasts while her pocketbook was open, humiliated, not for her participation in the filthiness, but for being caught and found out. You would have had to fix my face and box me six feet if Rev's mama ever caught me eating snake. I sighed from the bottom of my being—it just meant more prayer over my boys was necessary.

I recall how faithful my parents were in trying to get my hip healed. They recruited every reverend in shouting distance to pray over me. One young preacher had fire in his hands; one had ice. An older, granddaddy type said, "If it don't work, at least God gave her the blessing of beauty." Still, the feverish, knife-pained nights drew on, and Mama knelt at my bed, whispering, "By his stripes, you are healed," as fast and as fervently as her tongue would allow. In the memory, I realized mothers were always receptacles, always supplicants. Yes, Lord, I said, sinking down to my prayer rug, more conversation with you will fix it.

1-961018

Bird bones under brown skin. She was a seventh grader and hot in the ass, one of them girls that could break out to dancing any minute. He would see her and her friends in front of the building in the morning, spreading their legs and humping the air when the duty teachers weren't looking. He could hear them cackling like hens as they tried to outdo each other to show off. He knew they popped more when they thought he was watching. When she approached him at the homecoming dance, he could tell she was fast but scared. She came over and kind of stuck her butt out on him and ran off, giggling. The next time she tried it, he grabbed on to her and held her by her waist.

She was shaking a little as he started to move with her. When he bent down and said something in her ear, she smiled and relaxed. By the end of two slow songs in a row, he was ready for something else. The plan was that she would go out first, and he would follow shortly after, and they would meet down at the riverbank to mess around. He heard a series of cute, little sneezes before seeing her narrow, jacketed back, as she stood huddling herself. The Red Panther River sounded and smelled brown. Ghostly patches of trees gossiped at the water's edge. It was much darker down there than at street level, but just across the muddy river, you could see the lights of downtown. He took her by the hand and led her to the Canoe, an enlarged replica of the ones used by the Choctaw.

"So what you want to talk to me about, boy? It's freezing out here."

Her plump lips were jumping like crazy, and he began to rub his hands up and down her arms to warm her. He leaned down to fasten his mouth on hers. All she wanted to do was keep on kissing, but he had gotten aroused, and there was nothing left to it but to lay her down.

"What's this?" he asked, sticking his hand under her miniskirt.

"Ion know, boy, but you better stop."

But his fingers soldiered on. Her scrubby hair was parted deep on the left and had been painfully brushed and slicked down to the right. He hated when girls did this shit to their heads. It made him think of Camels and Colt 45, maybe a quick bendover under the Fourth Street bridge. He didn't know how he knew to associate those things with this hairdo, nor how he knew to drive her legs apart in this way, but he was doing it, fighting even as her bony knees pushed back.

Her panties were scratchy and fancy. Harlot red. It clicked in his head. She wore these, so he could do this, and at first, he held her shoulders down with his hands, but he soon realized his weight would do. This was her idea, what she wanted. She wasn't a virgin, was far from it. Cold sweat crinkled under his clothes. His body was blossoming, his middle was exploding. He felt outrageously good and gross at the same time. When he finished, he pulled her to her feet and helped her out of the Canoe. He brushed the leaves out of her hair, but she would have to wash it, which was good, he thought; she needed to get some of that gel out anyway. He untwisted her skirt and put her back together, but still she looked sort of stunned, like a little kid that had gotten their first real ass whipping. He felt like the parent, too—slightly sorry but also slightly smug for getting his point across.

"You love me, girl? You love me?"

Trembling like a sparrow, she nodded. He gave her a ten-dollar bill, a peck on the lips.

2

*I'm just a nobody trying to tell everybody about
somebody who can save anybody.*

FROM THE MINISTER'S DESK
Sabre J. Winfrey

June 11, 2000

MORNING MESSAGE: How to Deal with the Fools in Your Life

SCRIPTURAL BACKGROUND: "A whip for the horse, a bridle for the donkey, and a rod for the fool's back." Proverbs 26:3 NKJV

SABRE POINTS: The book of Proverbs illustrates many definitions of foolishness. What are some of them?_____

_____

_____

What does the Bible say about the Christian suffering fools?

_____

_____

How does the Word teach the Christian to avoid foolish behavior?_____

_____

_____

_____

The _____ of the Lord is the beginning of

_____

_____ .

DIAMOND

I spent most of Wednesday curled in bed with the covers over my head. I didn't have much of an appetite for anything but sad songs and thinking too hard. Seemed like I loved the sadness— maybe it loved me, too, and that was why it kept seeking me out because surely this heavy, throbbing, sinking, elastic sensation was the one I had known more than any other in my short life. I had a handful of friends and an extended family through Maggie, but it was with Wonder I truly felt I belonged to someone again. What happened with the First Lady walking in on us led me to believe what we had was destroyed. How could either of them respect me after that? The relationship was yet another thing to be lost.

The last place I lived with my mama and siblings was room 106 at the Sunflower Court Inn. They had remodeled and renamed the place, but the way it used to be stayed in my dreams and in the spaces between those dreams. The cool, slick bedspread, the damp woodsy smell, the ripeness of unwashed adults. I felt my brothers and sister, too, not just saw them in the eye of my mind—I sensed them individually but also as the unit we were at that time, a wholeness I had not felt since then. Sometimes, I wondered if my siblings remembered those days as vividly, or if they even cared to.

I could see Yancey on the floor of the room, scowling and bobbing to his headphones. Although he was the oldest at fourteen, Cricket, thirteen, was the bossiest. I was eight; Popeye, the baby, was six and curled at the foot of the bed away from us because nobody liked to hear him sucking his fingers. He was stout and red, the most savage of us if provoked. But mostly, we tried to get along. I was curled into the warm crescent Cricket's body made; the bedspread was doubled over on us. On the TV, an insurance salesman from Florida was beating the stew out of his competition on *Wheel of Fortune*. Our room was on the riverside; in an alcove next to our door was the ice machine and a temperamental drink machine. At all times of day and night, people could be heard cursing and cajoling the machine, until finally there was the satisfying thud of a can or the last, defeated thump of a foot. Inside the room, the four of us would try not to imagine the fizz of sugar water in our mouths. That day, a big car groaned its way to a stop outside. You could tell the door was long by the depth and length of the squeal. Yancey leapt over to the window and, shivering, peered out of the blinds and then over to us.

"Popeye's daddy out here with some lady."

Then Popeye's daddy was there, swinging open the door, sending in a patch of unexpected, warm light. We squinted at him; he had a bag of groceries in each arm, and he was without Mama even though they had left the room together several hours ago.

"Your mama is gone," he'd announced.

All four of us jumped to arms at the same time, all talking. Me and Cricket lurched off the bed. Popeye jumped up, his hands in fists. Yancey's skinny shoulders bristled. Popeye's daddy stepped around him and set the bags on the battered table. He snatched his duffel bag from the side of the bed him and Mama shared and began rooting around the room for his things.

"What you mean gone?" Cricket broke through.

"G-O-Gone," he said. "What part you don't understand?"

Yancey jumped in. "What do you mean gone? Where she gone?"

Me and Popeye stood aghast, gripped each other's hands.

"I don't know. She just told me she was tired and she'd be back if she got back."

For a moment, no one said anything, me specifically because it sounded like something Mama would say.

"Yancey, go get that watermelon out the back seat."

Yancey didn't leave. "Tell us where our mama at, nigga!"

"Boy, go get that damn watermelon before I slap the spit out of you."

Cricket gave me her bravest smile, rubbed up and down my back.

"My mama just wouldn't leave us like that," she said.

"Now yall know your crazy-ass mama," said Popeye's daddy from the bathroom.

He emerged with soap and towels. He ran his hand over the bedspread once more, peeked in the last nightstand. Then he walked his stiff-legged walk past all of us without looking even at Popeye.

"Yall keep that lunch meat and that juice in the cooler."

It was the last thing he said to us before he peeled out for good. He hadn't even taken Popeye or said anything special to him.

When I got out of my head, my heart didn't seem to be beating like normal, like remembering took part of me with the visit. I walked around the house, touching everything. I needed someone to hold me down, but Maggie was at work, and I wouldn't call Wonder. I was embarrassed, yes, but to be honest, I also felt betrayed, like he'd led me into that, like he had to know. And maybe that was what I sometimes thought about my mother, dead or alive, wherever she might be, that she delivered us into this: a lifetime of isolation, of wanting so bad that it hurts. I returned to my room, fell into a deep, dreamless sleep. In the early morning, I discovered Maggie face down on her bed. Carefully, I pulled her shoes off and covered her. She had left a note on the kitchen table, reminding me to wake her before *General Hospital*.

PRISCILLA

I washed down my pill with a swig of Jack, all the while thinking how I couldn't wait until the end of July, when football practice started again. But that was a whole month away, and the boy had been sticking close to home since the incident. I still didn't want to really talk to or look at him. But I couldn't help but notice him at the piano, playing and singing "Revelation 19" beautifully. Both he and Trey had perfect pitch. I wandered into the parlor, watching him from the doorway. He stopped when he saw me.

"Do you remember?" I asked.

"I'm sorry, Mama."

"You and your brother sang this, and you—six years old—with better pitch than Melvistine and all of them up there in the sanctuary choir. Lord, the church was on fire when yall sang that song. I can still feel the shivers up my spine."

I walked toward him, seeing him as he was then, my sweet baby boy with the anointed voice.

"Mama, listen," he said.

Even though my lips were numb, I picked up where he left off and played and sang myself, "For the Lord our God is Almighty, and the Lord our God is omnipotent!"

"Mama, listen."

My hands were in the air. "You hungry, baby?"

"Naw, Mama, I want to talk to you. I want to explain."

But I kept singing and ended up getting happy and the boy had to help me to a seat because the tears were streaming down my face. The strangest thing crossed my mind; at one time, there had been as many as three ding-a-lings in me—when the daddy was pointing up and the twins were pointing down. Crazy, huh? That should have toughened me in some way; instead, it rendered me weaker, more womanly. Maybe it was just Rev had done that. If there was anything he hated, it was when a woman bucked up like a man.

"I'll knock her flat," he'd say.

Of course, other women had five boys, but most of them had had girls, too, and girls would do work, not just make it. Every pregnancy, I dreamed of a tall, straight-legged daughter with lovely waves of dark hair and her daddy's wide nose that I had to remind her to pull up into shape. Manny was staring at me like a stranger when he brought me a handkerchief. I wiped my tears and was relieved when he went away and even more relieved when I heard his truck pull off. I hoped he'd go and let off some steam and release his need to talk to me about this thing. It was unnecessary, and I wouldn't understand. Don't get me wrong, I wasn't naïve or old-fashioned. I understood teen-aged urges were natural, but I couldn't shake the energy that radiated off of him, and it didn't feel playful and curious at all. It felt nuclear, dangerous, like someone I didn't and couldn't ever know.

DIAMOND

By Saturday morning, I managed to drag myself out to the porch for some fresh air. I sat on the metal rocker with my knees hugged up to my chest, looking and feeling like the orphan I was. It had been three days since the situation with the First Lady, and I missed Wonder, but I hated him a little, too. I desperately wanted someone to talk to about everything that had happened, but for the summer, my friend Bunny was working at Fred's and taking a class out at the college. She was always busy, and I didn't want her to flat out tell me she didn't want to hear the foolishness, and besides, she didn't care for Wonder, never had. Anybody else I could call would be fake and probably wishing for me and Wonder's downfall in the first place.

A gaggle of giggles interrupted my thoughts: the neighborhood girls assembling to Double Dutch with somebody's mama's phone cords. Did I ever laugh like that? Was I ever so free? The turners got the ropes going. I watched the first jumper dodge and then dance her way into the ropes, and when she caught a rhythm, a second joined her. They managed to be both wild and easy as they chanted: *G.I., gypsy, Muhammad Ali, who on Earth will your boyfriend be?* They weren't that much younger than me, but I felt ages older, maybe light-years. Old enough that a future I wasn't ready for was staring me in the face.

I was going into my senior year, and I had never been particularly good at school, not because I was dumb, but because I always had bigger shit to worry about. At least school was something consistent to do. It was scary to think that before this time next year, I would be graduating, and then what? College? A trade? I didn't even know what I was interested in. I wasn't one of those kids who had the luxury of knowing what was next. All the time I was growing up, when I imagined the future I was supposed to care so much about, I saw blackness, not like death, but nothingness. A childhood of instability meant I knew I couldn't call it, and I was a fool if I thought I could. The screen door opened, and Maggie's scent of bergamot and Obsession greeted me before she came into view. She had beautiful maroon skin and doorknob cheekbones, and my mind would not suppress the stubborn idea that she looked just like my mother—even though I knew that couldn't be possible.

"You good?"

She placed her hand on top of the fuzzy cornrows she'd done for me the other day.

"Yes, ma'am," I said, "just thinking."

"Something in particular?"

"My future and stuff, just stuff like that."

"Is it about that boy? Did he do something to you?"

"We good," I said. "I'm good, Ma."

Maggie started scratching my scalp with the tip of her fingernail, maybe at a patch of dandruff. It relaxed me, but I was somewhere else, too, somewhere all alone, despite her closeness.

"I was thinking of getting a job, doing something," I mumbled.

"If you ready and you want to, but your job is to be a kid. You've had a lot of loss and a lot of things you have to reckon with someday. A job will be there when it's time—a job, a boy, whatever it is you thinking you want, it all will be there at its proper time."

She was looking straight in my face, but I was a master at not giving anything away.

"Let's do something during my vacation. We can go eat— wherever you want. We can finally run to that new shopping center in Robinsonville."

"It's cool," I said.

What that meant I didn't know, but it seemed to work for her. She was watching the Double Dutch, now, too.

"Them girls got it going on," she said. "I used to could jump so high my knees hit my ears, but time does you dirty."

It made me laugh. She popped a kiss on my cheek and left for work. It wasn't her fault that I was always going to feel like an outsider. That's why I loved what I had with Wonder so much; it was like we were creating something all our own, something I inherently belonged to. I waited a few minutes and then went into my backpack for my little baggie of weed and lit up in the privacy of the backyard. Wonder hated narcotics, so I would never let him know I smoked or be around him high. The weed was hitting off-rip. I felt better immediately. I got to wishing I was like him, one of those kids with the whole world at their hands. He had so many options he took it casually.

Like he told me he had been asked to sing at his godsister's wedding in December, but he didn't know if he wanted to. If I had a voice like his, I would sing the phone book, the stuff on the cereal box, besides being on the *Apollo* and *Star Search*. The McGlowns were going to pay him and everything. I had never been to a wedding in my life, but I knew that Vicky Mc-Glown's would be a grand one to start with. He hadn't yet said anything about taking me with him, and I didn't have anything decent to wear if he asked. Maybe he would buy me a dress— like we were in *Pretty Woman*, minus anyone being a hooker, of course.

We were all due some good times, some good stuff. The last couple of years had been crazy for everybody, not just me. Folk called it the Reaping Season. Rev. Winfrey would say stay prayed up because every day people die that aint never died before. The wildest part was that it wasn't old people. Mrs. Kathareen's husband wasn't but thirty-one when he got killed in that accident. Mrs. Fox down the block had lost two great-grandsons to an epic gang battle at the car wash on Is-saquena, while rocking steadily through the deadly period on her porch, staring through the skim over her eyes and skeeting tobacco spit into a Folgers can. Another neighbor lost a half-grown granddaughter in the crossfire from that same battle. The white kids were sitting three to a cab in pickup trucks and flipping them like flapjacks every other weekend, and the city had to institute a curfew to contain it all.

After Kimmie passed of the leukemia, her mother brought over a big pile of her clothes, none of which I could ever make myself wear. If death was contagious, it stood to reason that wearing the garments of the recently departed was a sure way to catch it. Kimmie had been brave and sick forever, so at least she knew she was going to die. The others were surprised with the news. At this point, my high turned into bugging. I wondered if I would die young. Dying young made you a legend, but I decided I wanted no part of it. I worried about Maggie, too. What if she had a heart attack while trying to hoist Mr. Ringo up to change his diaper? Or what about that dream Wonderboy had where he was looking at himself in his coffin, naked but for his jersey?

I was terrifying myself. To calm down, I returned my thoughts to the wedding. In my fantasies, the dresses I wore varied, but my hair was always slicked back like Sade's. Wonder would not be able to keep his eyes off of me. *May I have this dance?* he would ask. Somebody would mistake us for the bride and groom. Mrs. Chow would bake the cake. It would be cloud-soft and so delicately sweet it would get lost in the warmth from my mouth. People would cut and eat from it all night, and it would never run out. But then I remembered what had happened and that I was mad at him. So I rolled up again, knowing it wasn't the high I wanted.

The next evening after church, the phone rang. I knew it was him, but I refused to answer, despite accidentally smiling at him in Sunday school. Maybe fifteen minutes later, I heard his beeps outside. I was prepared to act mad when I flung the door open, but he came up the walkway, so handsome and apologetic that my anger just evaporated, and I went into his arms and stayed a long time.

"You wanna go driving?"

"Yep," I said. Too eager, but I didn't care.

I grabbed my purse, locked the door, and hopped in his truck. We jetted down number 9, and he stopped us on the shoulder of Money Road, so we could trade places. Long and straight, a split of gray in the endless green of cotton and soybean, it was remote, perfect for driving lessons. Wonder was a thorough and patient teacher, even when I gunned the gas accidentally before putting the truck in drive. I flinched when I did it, but he urged me to start again. He didn't like that I flinched; he'd never hurt me.

He told me that Rev used to hit his mama. Not beat her, mind you, but he would smack her once in a while. His daddy said sometimes a woman needed a little attitude tune-up, but there was something wrong with your manhood if you had to beat on her all the time. Wonder said you shouldn't have to hit your woman at all. The threat of you should be enough. His words made me warm all inside, made me never want to be away from him. I loved how safe he made me feel.

PRISCILLA

I wiped down the stove, watching from the corner of my eye as Manny just picked over the tasty and nutritious breakfast I had prepared. The recesses of my mind were still occupied with trying to figure out how in the world he had come to be doing whatever it was he was doing. I knew Maggie's girl had come from troubled circumstances. Was it her idea? None of the boys but Mack had ever walked in on Sabre and me in the middle of any sort of marital relations—but Mack had always been rash, and he learned his lesson about barging in. Had Manny picked this habit up from one of his brothers? Or could he have seen his daddy with one of his "friends"? It certainly seemed like a shenanigan Sabre might participate in. My problem was less with the act itself than the energy he'd exuded. I heard his chair dragging and him scraping his plate into the trash. I put more elbow grease into cleaning the stove.

"You got enough?"

He mumbled something and was gone from the room. In his absence, I kept attempting to catalog his traumas. I finally settled on Sam; maybe this had something to do with that. The runt of a litter of pups I bought off the side of the highway, Sam was a weenie dog—sturdy, friendly, and he loved the boys as much as they loved him. Rev, on the other hand, had several issues with Sam. For one, he wasn't too keen on his boys playing with an animal shaped like a ding-a-ling. For two, the dog liked to stand on the back of the couch and bark out of the window. For three, he occasionally had a problem with bodily functions in the house. That was what ticked Rev off for the last time, when he stepped his Daniel Green slipper into a pile of dog poop in the study. He whacked Sam with the shoe until the dog wailed with great sorrow.

"Calm down, Sabre," I kept trying to soothe him. "Please."

But he was heaving like a monster as he dragged the poor animal into the backyard to chain him up. After the air in the house had settled, I shooed the boys out of the way so I could cook. Couldn't have been an hour later, I was rinsing my knife when I looked out of the window and saw Sam hung up on the side of the fence with Manny stricken in front of him. He must've gone out to try to make the dog feel better. I slammed the knife down, darted out the back door and across the yard to Sam, whose legs were doing a jerky bicycle, just shy of the ground where they needed to be.

"Ma," my boy called.

It was a cold, high sound of pain and bewilderment that could still yank me out of sleep. I unraveled Sam from his circumstance, released the clasp on his leash. He fell like a log and tumbled onto his side, where he quickly gave up the ghost. I swept Manny up in my arms and buried his head in my chest. I had on a boatneck; his tears and my tears slid down my skin and into my shirt. Fear ran cold in me when I saw Rev staring at us from the study. His evil fell on me like a blanket. Later, I found the boys in the twins' bedroom, looking like orphans.

"Mama, do Sam got a soul?" Moshe asked.

"Son, if His eye is on the sparrow, you know He got Sam in His bosom, too."

That seemed to be enough for them, whatever it meant to

me at the time. Neither me nor the boys had an appetite after that. I heard Rev moving around, and I guessed he was disposing of the remains. I never asked where he took the dog, but by the time he got back, I had moved a great deal of my stuff into the guest bedroom. I knew and expected certain things from him, for he was nothing but a man, but that kind of cruelty I didn't know how to address or reconcile. Now I only went into his bedroom to change his sheets.

I kept thinking about the status of my marriage as I ran the vacuum over the large rug in the den. Normally, a Black woman could depend on something like diabetes or colon or prostate cancer to put rest to a problem husband. Rev, unfortunately, didn't too much care for salt, fried food (unless it was fresh caught out of a river), or sweets (except for my butter roll). Also too, he ran regularly with his football boys or went to Bear's Boxing Gym. He had even done a commercial for them. "Fight like Jacob," he'd said, and thrown out several punches and pointed straight at the screen, smiling with those gapped teeth. Before we got married, we had sat in the just-darkness on my parents' porch, and I had pressed my tongue against that space even though my mama said a man with a gap in the middle of his mouth is a liar before the living God. And you know what, my mama was right. But I came to discover he was less a lie-dropper than an actual outright lie himself. His very being was a lie.

What I was looking forward to when he died was getting to manage the world's last view of his earthly form. I would put him in a hell-red suit and sing a solo wearing my auburn fox stole whether it was July or January. And although Rev's monies would be there still to support me, I would be justified in remarrying because of my fairly young age, my late husband's stature, and my holy reserve, provided that my new husband was older than I and at least the stature of my late husband. Dr. Booker had not remarried since his wife had passed, and just last week when I'd run into him at the post office, he had come up behind me and said, "You know you were supposed to be mine, Cilla." He was handsome, if on the rotund side, but I could work with him. If I died, Kathareen would be in here inside of a week "helping" Rev to get by.

Speak of the devil, and he'll come home from the barbershop early. I heard his car pull into the driveway while I was in the laundry room, and I didn't move until he entered the house. He looked good, I had to admit, in slacks and gators, and one of his older smocks that I had embroidered when we first got married.

"Hello, husband," I said.

He eyed me suspiciously. "What all did you put in them muffins this morning, Cilla? Seems like my stomach's been bothering me all day."

"Maybe it aint your stomach, Rev; maybe it's your conscience. We still haven't talked about me finding that foundation on your shirt. Is it that Fashion Fair Kathareen cakes on? That would figure . . ."

"Quit, Cilla, just quit. I told you I don't feel good."

But I didn't want to quit. I wanted him to feel bad like I did.

"You think your sons have no idea about your real lifestyle, but I guess it don't matter to you what you teach them."

"To woman he gave a womb, and to man he gave

dominion—that's what I teach my boys because that's what the living Word say."

With that, a full-blown picture of Manny standing over that girl was again in my head. Dominion—that's what that was about, not love or even pleasure—it was dominion, and that's what bothered me. Just then, he came down the stairs. He had on blue basketball shorts and a mesh jersey with his backpack slung over his shoulder. Rev appraised his growing physique. He was my second-huskiest boy, besides Mack, heavier than his father. Rev was no fool; he had long ago stopped trying to rule them by the strength of his hand.

"Go easy on them weights, son," he said. "You a quarterback. You don't want to put on all that bulk and become clumsy and slow. Quarterbacks aint gone be able to dance in that pocket no more; the future of the position is mobile."

"Yes, sir," Manny said with a salute.

The daddy pulled the boy into his arm and knuckled across his head, mussing his hair. The daddy was taller, but the boy was broader.

DIAMOND

After Popeye's daddy left us at the Sunflower, the three of us had a conference about our situation. Yancey had already figured out I would get adopted because I was pretty, and Popeye because he was still young. Cricket's folks would come get her, and Yancey—well, nobody adopted fourteen-year-olds. He would be in foster care or a group home until he aged out. If

Mama was gone, it was only a question of how soon we would be caught and split up. Popeye was rocking and rolling in his sleep, and I suggested we release him from whatever was bothering him.

"Let him stay sleep. He don't need to hear this," Cricket said.

Though in the moment, Cricket sounded thirteen going on thirty, I still thought Popeye needed to know what could await him, so he wouldn't be surprised. Cricket smelled like fear and the rose dust that she always managed to get from somewhere. Every morning, she opened the tin, dunked the puff, and brushed various parts of her body with the powder, leaving white scuffs and the aroma of soft old women on her clothes. She had done it this morning, too. The smell made me want to cry, but neither one of them was crying, so I couldn't. Yancey came to the bed on my other side, and we stooped as if we were holding the same concrete slabs on our backs.

"I honestly think he deaded Mama and dumped her somewhere," he said in a way that said that was that.

"Mama aint dead," I snapped. "And I know she wouldn't just up and leave us, neither."

"Why would he up and say that then? He wouldn't have said nothing at all if he didn't know for sure she was gone forever."

I said, "That don't mean nothing. Mama's not gone. I know she aint. She knows we can't do nothing without her."

"One of us could go look for her at Toronto Jack's or Lucky's," Cricket said.

Yancey put one hand on top of my head and the other on Cricket's. His palm was not big, but it was reassuring. He said, "Imma run upstairs to see if Ms. Yvonne has talked to her."

Ms. Yvonne in 202 was Mama's cigarette and Spades friend. It was almost nine o'clock on a Friday night, so we knew she had been drinking for three hours at least. The way Yancey had come back, with lipstick all over his jaw and seeped through with tobacco smoke, confirmed it. Although he had no valuable news about Mama, someone at Ms. Yvonne's had gifted him with a zipper bag of penny candy, the chewy kind with white wrappers and tangy-sweet, unidentifiable fruit flavors. With quick fingers, Cricket spilled the bag open and split them out in three piles; she did this because whenever we had a communal bag of something, she said I became infected with the reachitis. She only saved two for Popeye, because, with a mouth full of welfare teeth, he didn't need much candy anyway. I filled my mouth with four of my pieces and began a gloppy chewing. Yancey wanted to leave Popeye behind, sleeping, but Cricket said that if he woke up, he would wake up screaming and go crazy, and so it was decided that because it was already dark, we would all go, that somebody would just have to snatch us all.

It was early August, a walking night, breezy and not too warm. Rain threatened. The Soap Opera was closed tight. Toronto Jack's was just a couple of blocks down, and across from it was the Lucky Lounge. It was early, and Cricket ducked in and out of both of those places with no news for us. She had checked the bathrooms and everything. On the way back, between Toronto Jack's and the Soap Opera, the rain started. We skittered down the sidewalk and stopped under the sloping roof of a carless house. Popeye whined for more candy, but working steadily, I was down to two pieces, which I collapsed on my tongue as we watched the rain sluice down. I swallowed; my mouth was mucky from old sugar. Back at home, we had lunch meat and thick cheese and the rest of the Little Debbies when we'd dried off. Cricket read to us out of the *Reader's Digest* about a man who survived a plane crash off the coast of Nova Scotia.

"I aint never getting in no plane," Popeye had said.

Unruly breasts. She was first-seat saxophone in the band, one of the quiet types you had to watch out for because they were undercover whores. But she was kind of cute: two big white teeth up front, deep rusty skin, and thick hair that she kept in ponytails. They met at the library to work on an honors English project. He came in late, straight from football practice, wearing low-slung sweatpants and a T-shirt that sunk in the ridges of his belly. He perceived the electric of her body when he got close to her. They stayed at the library until it closed. He carried her stack of books and placed it beside her on the stone planter.

Her big sister was supposed to pick her up, and he didn't want to leave her alone and unsafe. Since she wouldn't wait in his car with him, they sat outside the building and chatted about the weather; how the Olmec statues in history class looked just like Black people; and their favorite movies. A half hour later, her sister still having never arrived, she accepted his offer to drive her home, but first, he had to run into Fred's dollar store for Epsom salts because he *had* just gotten out of practice. He lobbed his purchases in the back seat, and as if by remote control, he reached across her lap and reclined her seat as far as it would go. A streetlight beamed like a spotlight.

"You got a mustache," he said, laying his finger there.

But quickly, he redirected, began fiddling with this complicated bra and undershirt system she had going on, but determined, he figured it out, and was rewarded with the plumpest, most unruly breasts he'd ever come across. Her fight collapsed against the force of his mouth on her skin. His teeth throbbed and dug into brown flesh.

3

*I'm just a nobody trying to tell everybody about
somebody who can save anybody.*

Sabre J. Winfrey

June 18, 2000

MORNING MESSAGE: You Can Put a Pig in a Wig, but It's
Still a Pig.

SCRIPTURAL BACKGROUND: "The woman was arrayed in purple
and scarlet and adorned with gold and precious stones and
pearls, having in her hand a golden cup full of abominations and the filthiness of her fornication. And on her
forehead a name was written: MYSTERY, BABYLON THE GREAT,
THE MOTHER OF HARLOTS AND OF THE ABOMINATIONS OF THE
EARTH." Revelation 17:4-5 NKJV

SABRE POINTS: Why should the Christian guard against getting caught up in appearances?_____

_____

How can the Christian recognize the golden cups of abomi-
nation he carries?_____

_____

Why is the discernment of the Spirit so important in these
cases?_____

_____

What is the ultimate consequence of seeking worldly ap-
proval, as opposed to God's?_____

_____

PRISCILLA

Manny dropped me off at the salon to get my hair done for the Saints vs. Sinners Banquet. It had been a couple of months since I sat in C. Michael's chair, and he had a fit over the state of my roots. By the time he finished, I had lost the grays, five inches of hair, and about ten years. I loved the bangs, and the rollers had just given it so much body. It felt light, just right for the summertime.

"It's a little young," the boy said when I got in.

"What does that mean?"

"Daddy won't like it."

"I like it," I said. "It only matters if I like it."

But catching the color in full sun had alarmed me. What I thought was copper was way too bright, like I had flames on my head. At home, I went straight upstairs and into my closet, where I took a drink and wrapped my hair and put a scarf on, hoping somehow it would tone the color down before tonight. I decided then to pull my vestments for the banquet to clear my head. I had been asking Bertha all week which ticket she was buying, but she had played it coy. Me on the other hand, I was wearing cream, so folk could see where I stood right away. My new suit was lace, with a jacket that cut around to frame my hips, and a knee-length skirt with a little kick train at the back. I pulled out my cream panama hat, just in case I changed my mind about liking my hair. I was pretty sure I was going to go with my mint silk shell underneath the jacket, but I didn't know whether I was going to hit them with the gold pumps or the emerald peep-toes. I hunted through dozens of clear shoeboxes until I had both pairs, and both just looked scrumptious. All I needed were my emerald earrings to set it off.

They were missing from the tray on my vanity. I peeked behind and underneath it, and on the floor nearby in case I had knocked them over, but they weren't there. I tore the place up trying to find them. I sat on the chaise at the foot of my bed, forcing my frantic mind to retrace my steps. I had the earrings on at the city beautification planning meeting Sabre and I attended the night before, and when I took them off, I set them in that dish before I got in the tub. I was absolutely sure that was what happened, but the earrings weren't there. Nor were they in my jewelry box, pocket, purse, or anywhere else in the house. Since Sabre rarely climbed the stairs, I went into the hall and yelled for the boy. Several moments later, he appeared. I directed him to sit because I didn't prefer to look up at my sons.

"What's up, Ma?"

"Don't 'what's up' me. Have you seen my earrings?"

"What earrings?"

"My emeralds with the circle of diamonds around them. They were in the little dish on my vanity."

"I don't know what you talking about, Ma."

"You do know what I'm talking about. I've had the earrings your whole life. They're green with diamonds! And I put them in that dish, and now they're nowhere to be found."

"Ma, what Imma do with your earrings?"

"Well, who got them then? Did your little girlfriend steal them? Do I need to call and ask Maggie?"

"Ma, that girl doesn't have your earrings. I haven't even seen her since then," he said.

"How I know that? You had her here under my nose in the first place—doing whatever shenanigans yall was doing. Any hussy that will just lay there like that will steal, too!"

"You trippin, Ma," he said.

He sighed like he knew better than me, which infuriated me.

"I'm tripping?" I said. "I'm tripping?!"

Before I knew it, I had smacked him—I think I was as shocked as he was. I had little validity in the hitting arena because Sabre had been the disciplinarian. He would let their sins tally, bend them over in the backyard, and light their little behinds and scrotums up with a leather strap. The twins were meek and mild, Ivy had never been much trouble, and Manny did most everything right. Mack, my untamed one, was the only one to take lashes like an ox. I had rarely hit them, and here Manny was, glaring at me like I was a stranger he didn't like the smell of. His eyes were so like mine, situated in a face so like his daddy's, but his temperament was all his own, something I'd never seen. He stood.

"Where are you going?"

"Doing bleachers."

"You need to go to your room. You never sit still. You doing too much."

"Like father, like son," he scoffed.

"Well, I would hope not," I said.

When he was out of sight, I did take medicine, but even it wasn't enough to calm me down as I ransacked the house for my earrings.

～～～

"Get a move on, Cilla," came Sabre's voice from the bottom of the stairs.

If he had been deciding on which one of them country-ass suits to wear, I would have been expected to wait all day. I sighed and slid out the giant hairpins holding my wrap in place. Delicately, I unmolded it, combing down my bangs and letting the rest fall to my shoulders. I was digging my new hair, but then at the last minute, I decided it was too much and put the hat on. Sabre shouted up again.

"Cilla, if you riding with me, you'd better get to getting."

"Give me a minute! Damn," I said.

I put the finishing touches on my makeup and went ahead with the green peep-toes to give the outfit a little more pop because the pearls I picked as a substitute for my emeralds just weren't doing it for me. Let it be known, I still looked damn good, though; let it be known, and let it be said. I tipped down the stairs like a Maltese kitten.

"Wipe off some of that blush" was what he said when he saw me. "It's unholy."

I started to just go back up the stairs and stay home like I'm sure he wanted. But I wasn't going to give him the satisfaction. I simply looked him up and down, taking in the white double-breasted monstrosity he wore, walked past him, and waited for him to open the door for me. One thing he had to do for the public is treat me like the lady I was. We shared a silent ride to the church, but it wasn't charged or cold; it was just us. When

59

we got to the Seals, he beelined for his study to spend a few moments preparing for his grand appearance.

I walked into the fellowship hall alone, looking at everything and spreading around a couple of how-you-doings before settling down. Dora and them had really done a nice job on the decorations. A wide burgundy runner split the room in stark halves, which you weren't supposed to cross until after benediction, when salvation breached the gap. Hell, on the left, was lit in red-and-black crepe flames with a few giant splashes of white lightning to illuminate the doom that awaited the unrepentant sinner. The ticket to hell was ten dollars, and members of the sustenance ministry served the hell-raisers fried chicken / fish, spaghetti, coleslaw, dinner rolls, and devil's food cake. On the other side of the runner was heaven. Zion was decorated with tinfoil stars and tissue paper clouds; the ticket was fifteen dollars, in recognition of the higher cost of salvation, the fight and sacrifice, the struggle to get and stay righteous. On the menu was baked chicken / fish, mashed potatoes, green beans, salad, dinner rolls, and angel food cake.

Hell was packed, but there was only one full table in heaven. There sat a handful of church mothers, plus Melvistine, Brenda-Gale, and Hattie. Although I didn't want to, I had to sit with them. Loudmouthed Melvistine was running the conversation, going on and on about the Eastern Stars, when Bertha sashayed in, wearing the dress I told her to throw away after her mama's funeral. She aimed a little sheepish smile at me, but I made sure she saw me rolling my eyes good and hard. I should have known better, though—every year she bought a ticket to hell. She never could resist nothing fried. You could fry air and despair, and Bertha would want a piece. Applause sprung up out of nowhere, and I turned to see Sabre gliding through in that white suit. From somewhere, he'd acquired a silvery sparkly sash that he had fastened across himself. He strode over to the makeshift podium in front of the baptismal pool. His hands rose, and so did the church to its feet, and he officially opened the program.

"Heaven or hell: it's your choice," he said. "I think I'll say that again . . ."

These remarks weren't my work, but their resonance rippled through the crowd. I glanced at Sabre and then Bertha, who looked away. I was glad when the praise dance team came to the stage, so I could have a distraction. The blessed performance put me in a much better mood, but that didn't last long. Because here Katherine arrived in a skintight red dress and widow's veil, with some poor bald yak's hair hanging to her behind, and every eye beheld her.

DIAMOND

Wonder called me, agitated. He needed me right then, so I hopped in a sundress and combed my hair. Maggie had the kitchen smelling like coffee and warmth; she was taking something out of the oven. Although I was the better cook, and that wasn't saying much, on her days off she liked to experiment in the kitchen. When she saw me, she smiled and tilted the cookie sheet down so I could see. Big beige nuggets of something she tumbled onto a bed of paper towels.

"They're good—sausage scones," she said, "with biscuit mix and cheese—Bertha told me how to make them."

She picked one up and broke it open in front of my nose. Inside were flecks of meat and cheese. Though they looked like stones, these smelled pretty good, so I dropped two on a saucer.

"Where you headed to so early?"

"Job hunting. I really wanted to ride out to the casinos to fill out applications, but somebody here keeps telling me no."

"We're not that bad off that I have to send you up and down the road to the boat."

"I could make good money working at one of those buffets."

"Yeah, no—maybe try the day care or one of the fast-food places first," she said.

I bit into the crunchy ball. It was a bit dry, but the flavor was decent. I stopped chewing to give her a side-eye. Her hair was styled in the candy cane French roll she'd gotten done for the banquet, and she had on makeup and a crisp yellow shirt buttoned up to her chin.

"Where are you going is the real question here."

Her strong, bowed legs were shined up and on display in a denim skirt and espadrilles. She was pouring milk into my coffee, but she stopped and twirled around so I could see her from all angles.

"If you must know, Nosy Rosy, me and Dennis are riding to the Mall of Memphis."

She set the cup in front of me, but as she sat down, Manny's horn honked outside. I squeezed the rest of the last of my breakfast into my mouth and poured my coffee into a Styrofoam cup.

"Manny aint coming in?"

I shook my head and looped my sandal over my heel.

"I know he's got you spoiled and all, but we in a hurry today, Mama."

She filled a zipper bag of sausage balls that she pressed in my hand, and she followed me to the door, calling out to where he sat in his humming truck.

"I know your mama probably cooked this morning, but I sent you something to snack on," she said.

"Thank you, Ms. Maggie. I'll be over this evening or Monday morning to cut the yard."

"Thank you, Manny."

I was halfway down the steps, but I returned, put the food down, and unbuttoned the top three buttons of her shirt. She swatted me, rebuttoned one of them. Later, we would probably double back after she left, but for now, we were driving to our spot. We parked in the parking lot of the Rebel Cave and walked downhill toward the Red Panther River, sinking in its gray, fractured banks since the spring rains ended in April. A quarter of a mile later, we were at the Canoe, spreading out a blanket to cover its soft-rotting insides. Above us the determined traffic crossed the Fourth Street bridge. Around us the foggy sweetness of the magnolias drifted down, and the leaves and the trees and the shade and river together made a chummy smell. We arranged ourselves inside the Canoe; already, he was stroking himself. A tear blobbed in the corner of his bruised left eye. Only I knew this big boy-man was broken, and he just had to let whatever it was out of his system. I didn't want him wasting that stuff, though—I wanted it in me. My body wanted to grow huge with his child. I wouldn't dare say it, though. I couldn't say for sure what he'd think. He shuddered when he was empty and kissed my mouth. We slept a little and woke when the sun was too hot on our faces. We sat up, but neither of us made a move to leave. I kissed the bruise.

"You want to talk about it?" I asked.

"Not really," he said.

"That's cool."

"I bought you something," he said.

I was grinning so it seemed my face would crack. He gave the best gifts.

"Close your eyes," he said.

He took my hand and pressed small objects into it. I opened my eyes and was dazzled by brilliant gems in my hand.

"These look real," I said. "And real expensive."

"That's because they are. Put them on."

I was shocked: "I can't take these."

"Take them," he said, voice sounding hoarse. "Put them on."

I obeyed, pulled out my little compact mirror. To see them on me, flashing like green fire, was thrilling. I felt like somebody else, a princess. He helped me out of the Canoe, and I began to walk like one, like I had on a dress that trailed behind. He laughed, but I kept on, nose to the sky. As we came up to the sidewalk, chatty brown birds blocked our path.

"Look at them all in the way. Why are they walking when they can fly?" I asked.

"It takes a whole lot more energy to fly than to walk," he said, "and food is on the ground."

Suddenly he roared at the flock, sending them clacking and

fluttering. We drove toward State Street with his hand cradling my knee, and I felt so giddy, so girly, so soft even, when I knew I was none of those things. At the snack stand, he got us chili cheese fries and ice cream, and we sat under the big umbrella to eat and watch people.

A person aint always just shaped by the traumatic shit. Yes, I'd known plenty of that, but I had blinders on for the good shit, too. Like me as a person, besides this time with Wonder, my life was shaped most by the happy time in our house in the Brickyard. My mama had always been peculiar, but in those days, she was more so just quirky. When I think of that time, I first think of garbage trucks. Actually, I think of sleep first, tight and warm, curled under my window, and then the garbage truck, rattling and wheezing in the alley like some giant prehistoric metallic animal. And it's because shit was regular, you know, it happened at a time you could expect and you could plan around those regularities, and you didn't have to be afraid of the shifts. The shifts are what get you out of whack.

What got us out of whack was Mama's miscarriage.

It was after Popeye came.

Newcharles Powell Scott, called Popeye, was born on February 19, 1986, to Sonja Ann Bailey and Charles T. Scott, and afterwards, they got married. Mama had three children already, and everybody would ask her what she did to manage to get a man when she already had not one but three kids by different men. Charles was making good money at Cooper Tire, and Mama worked in the cafeteria at Eliza P. Walker. Each week, she brought home bags of yeast rolls and box after box of nearly expired school milk, which I enjoyed lining up at the bottom of the refrigerator. Although I didn't much like the appliances; they were a burnt color from the seventies, but they were really the only things I didn't like about our house. Outside was just enough yard for three kids to run circles in. The inside had foot-muffling brown carpet, a deep, peach tub with swans on the shower door, and permanent shadows from the high, square windows. The house always smelled like popcorn or Pine-Sol or the incense that would burn into a perfect cone of dust if you let it be, but I never could.

At the motel, shit was every whichaway. Things happened at their regular times in the Brickyard: school, Mama and Charles, and all kinds of music—J. Blackfoot, Aretha, Santana, Whitney. They went on a date every other Friday, leaving us with Jemima, his sister, who made us popcorn and Coke floats and let us watch movies until our eyes got grainy. We had the best Christmas ever in that house, and no one was mad that Popeye got the most stuff. I got a Baby in a Basket that cost $39.99 (I knew because I had circled it in the JCPenney Wishbook); the doll came in a white picnic basket that included her layette, diapers, bottles, and anything else you'd need to take care of her. The birth certificate, which I still have, read Cornelia Deborah.

How I Lost Baby Cornelia by Diamond Michelle Bailey: Once upon a time, the shit hit the fan. After Popeye, Mama lost a baby, and it very much troubled her that she had miscarried after having already delivered four healthy children. Shortly thereafter, Charles went to work tipsy and got a forklift driven through his leg. Life was quieter in the little house, still steady, but no date nights and no music, unless you counted their drumbeat arguments. One day after school, we came home to eviction: the sheriffs had spread our stuff out on the lawn without any care for us at all. Charles was on the striped love seat on the curb smoking a cigarette. In the five minutes it took him to run in the corner store down the street, somebody got his stereo, which he had tried to hide behind the bushes.

"Somebody had to have been somewhere watching, just waiting on me to leave," he said.

Evidently, somebody got Baby Cornelia, too. I searched and searched through our piles of stuff, but she was gone forever.

Wonder was shaking me. To my surprise, we were at the stand, having ice cream, and I was seventeen, not seven.

"Where were you?" he asked.

I smiled but said nothing at all. He was shaping me, this was shaping me.

PRISCILLA

After the banquet the night before, my pride wouldn't let me pull Bertha to the side and ask her if she had some fulfillments for a downhearted saint. I felt like she owed me for leaving me with Melvistine them by myself all evening, while she had a good ol' time bumping gums with the rest of the riffraff in hell. Part of me didn't blame her—if hell was the only option to avoid Melvistine and her cronies—but I digress. My pride didn't allow me to speak to her or anyone else at all afterwards, not even to say goodbye; I sat in the car while Rev hobnobbed and whatnot. Let them wonder why. I could not care less! And then that Kathareen, arriving late as if she was some kind of celebrity or something and gobbling up everybody's attention like an eclipse or a blackout or black hole—anything dark and hungry that ate up the light. Who did that hussy think she was? Between that and my missing earrings and this boy, an ugly, mean, heavy sensation wouldn't shake me loose.

I cleaned what was already tidy and then typed the program for church service. The work occupied me for a while, but this belief I was losing my handle on life crept into the corners of me. It didn't help that Rev had custody of my prescription, and Bertha wasn't answering her phone. When life got like this, bad things happened. Even the biggest, loosest rubber band has a point where it won't stretch no further. And if I popped, all people would do was call me ungrateful and undeserving, like last time.

It was '92–'93, and between all the football championship stuff, the Sing Tour being written up in the *Appeal* (with my words but without crediting me, as usual), and me teaching and working with five active boys, it's like one day, I just malfunctioned. According to the *Press Register*, I was detained by police and charged with public drunkenness, indecent exposure, and assault of a peace officer. Rest assured, the charges were false and exaggerated upon further by the bag-faced mouth of the South, who went around lying like I had a nervous breakdown and was shoplifting at the Liberty Cash.

First, we had enough money to buy that dingy store twice over, and second, where in the world would a woman of my petite stature hide a ham? Yes, I had on my sable mink—it was a mink type of day—beautiful, chilly, yellow, and so blue. No, it didn't matter what I had on underneath. And yes, I stood in the butcher shop of the Liberty Cash for quite some time, but I was not stealing; I was staring at the ham. The living pinkness captivated me, the luminous fat. It resembled something you could just go snatch off any human. I got to wondering if this was what Jesus meant by the remembrance of his body. And the fact that it made me ravenous wasn't lost to me, but the words I screamed there in the store were.

After that incident, I was forced to resign as instructor of choral music at Dominion Junior College, and my four private piano students dwindled to one, which had since dwindled to none. Rev was 4:30 hot. No telling what he told the boys; they seemed like they wanted nothing to do with me, especially the twins, who were in high school at the time. Instead of letting my actions ruin his reputation, Rev made me ask for prayer at the altar, like in those days when a fast girl or woman got pregnant out of wedlock and had to confess in the sanctuary. I became his cross to bear, strengthening his popularity. Who could blame him for chasing tail if his wife was crazy?

Of course, that was before fulfillments helped straighten my crooked rows. In the end, my life didn't miss a beat when I stopped working, and since I didn't have to get it out the mud like most women, no one had a bit of sympathy for me in the aftermath. What more could I ask for than a house full of handsome and healthy sons and a prosperous husband? Well, for one, I wanted my husband to be as good a man as he proclaimed himself to be, and for two, I wanted all of my sons to be the men I'd hoped they would be—not sneaky, freaky, lying copies of their father.

~~~~~

When my mood hadn't improved by early afternoon, I rode my bike by Bertha's house. Both her little putt-putt and her old man's Continental were pulled up in the yard, so I knocked on the door, but no one answered. Outside was too hot for the civilized, and here they were playing while I needed my fulfillment. Lord, I couldn't wait until the twins got out of medical school and could just prescribe they mama what she needed.

"Open the damn door, Bertha. I know yall in there."

I was embarrassed as hell, and Bertha Benny oughta be ashamed of herself, knowing she'd be the first person needing twenty dollars until payday. I had the stump to fit her rump if she just didn't jump, though. I huffed off the porch, rode home, swigged some Jack, not before seeing Ivy had come and dumped his laundry and left. I got them sorted and started, just to have something to do. I called upstairs for Manny, but there was no answer. His truck was in the alley, but Ivy's was gone, so I guessed they must be out somewhere together.

Later on, Rev came home in a good mood with dinner from Kemp's, knowing I love me a Kempburger. He read the news, but we ate together in the kitchen. He got me the pulled pork on a bun with grilled onions, coleslaw, and extra Madear sauce. I ate the whole thing, and I needed it after all that alcohol on an empty stomach. That night, when he was relaxing in the living room, I brought him his typed sermon in a manila folder. On the stereo was Al Green, but I couldn't tell right off if it was blues Al or church Al. Rev skimmed the sermon and then set the folder on the mahogany side table. With a corner of a smile on his face, he patted the space beside him on the leather sofa. He turned the volume on the stereo down and made a little crook in his arms for me. I went there, not knowing his motives, but I was touch-starved and made nostalgic by a barbecue sandwich.

His feet were long and slim and crossed on the coffee table. His legs were long; his thighs made hills under his pants. When we had first gotten together, I had kissed those thighs in gratefulness, in lust. He used to play in my hair. Did he love me like that still? Did it make sense for him to? I knew I loved him, even when I dumped the senna in his muffin batter a couple of weeks ago, and he had to come home early. Lord knows I didn't want to hurt him; I just wanted him to feel me.

On the radio, blues Al sang, "Make believe, make believe one mo time."

The next day, between Sunday school and church services, I went to fix the floral arrangement in the foyer. I was hitching up a lolling tulip when in stepped Maggie and her girl. Her hair was in a large, puffy bun at the top of her head, and she looked like she was carrying splashes of green light in her ears. My mouth flopped open. That boy had looked right in my eye and lied to me. She wouldn't have dared to wear them to church if she had stolen them. The two ducked in the ladies' restroom as all the heat of my body soared into my cheeks. Tackling the girl and snatching out my earrings wasn't appropriate for the place or time and pulling her to the side was out of the question. I knew I couldn't ignore Maggie and the child because the foyer was full, and everyone around here was so nosy. I could just hear somebody saying, "You know First Lady didn't speak to Maggie this Sunday," and somebody else would say, "Must have something to do with that boy. Wonder what's going on there."

I could choke Emanuel, but he and Ivy were already banging and clanging up front. I decided to quickly make my way up to my seat and just catch the girl after church. I kept shooting that boy glances, but he was avoiding my eyes. Lord, have mercy on the woman who marries him. Before I could contemplate this further, Bertha Benny sidled up to me, talking about how sorry she was she missed my call yesterday, but her sinuses was kicking her butt.

"Umph," I said.

"Girl, I didn't have nothing no way because Ty is tripping, as the kids say. He say we have to come to him from now on."

I rolled my eyes to the top of my head. If it wasn't one thing, it was six. The boys began to sing in earnest, causing the congregation to rise to worship. Lord, I loved Ivy's voice. He was the smallest of my boys, but he had the greatest vocal range. He could sing from that higher baritone all the way to a beautiful falsetto, which came from his diaphragm, unlike his father's, whose came from his throat. A clear, soaring scream erupted, the sign somebody was getting the Spirit already. As Bertha scurried off to do her usher board duty, I swiveled my head to a discreet angle to see who. Much to my holy chagrin, I see Kathareen bouncing around with her hands up. I rolled my eyes again.

Later, when services were over and Rev was at the station, Bertha picked me up to go to Tyrone's. On a regular day, he came to Bertha, who distributed to various outlets, which made it easy and prudent for me. When you were in as much pain as I was, though, you had to do what you had to do. I got in the car and witnessed Bertha in a headache-colored muumuu and penny loafers she had walked on the backs of. Her hair was wrapped up, and her ankles had not been oiled. I tugged at the slightest of creases in my linen dress and aimed the mirror down at my face to make sure all was as intended. My hair was perfect, and I had swept on a little more rouge because you never knew who was going to be where you were going—and here Bertha was looking like the last slave freed.

"Chile, you know you oughta be shame of yourself for stepping out your door looking like that," I said.

Bertha swiveled to face me, all the while bucking with her big old eyes.

"Four-one-one information: I done kept my old man for fourteen years, and he like me just fine. Besides, we just going to my brother's house. Whatever you wear to that infested hovel you likely to have to burn anyway."

And yall not married neither, I thought, but she was right about Tyrone's house. As we drove, I guessed she felt the need to try to get her lick back.

"I bet you and the Reverend is sad that none of your sons have got the call."

She said that because the call to the gospel normally came much younger in a family that was two generations in the cloth already; folk was saying that over there at Bethel AME, Bishop DeShazer's miraculous boy got the call when he was four, but the Lord hadn't said the same for any of ours.

"Bertha, you know I heard one too many people was lying and saying I was upset by that. I'm truly not. Yes, I would love for one or more of my sons to be a shepherd, but I know that that's not the only way they can serve God."

"Umph," said Bertha.

This was the first time I had gotten to use this answer I had been preparing, so I was glad when I saw it had the correct, humbling effect on her. I wished she hadn't asked me that because I had wanted to seek her counsel on Emanuel's lying and thieving behavior, but after my little speech, I didn't want to sully my boy's name. We pulled up to the side of the forsaken trailer where Tyrone lived with his Mexican woman. They had a prowling, growling, hissing-ass cat they called Barry. I hated cats, and to make matters worse, this one had the nerve to be missing big patches of fur and one whole eye. As we climbed the wopsided steps, my back and neck and legs felt electric in anticipation of Barry jumping out of nowhere. If cats became suicidal, surely, this one would be a candidate. What kept him hanging on? Certainly, if he were behind my back tires, I would not brake. Bertha banged on the door.

"Ty! Ty," she was yelling.

The Mexican woman opened the door. She had Kool-Aid-red hair and prehistoric heels grinding down the spines of her canvas shoes. The house smelled like death had visited, messed everything up, and made a sorry effort at cleaning up behind himself. Tyrone hobbled in from somewhere and planted himself on the blue plaid couch. He had the kind of black-eyed pea hair that should always be kept as short as possible, and his shirtless chest was concave. The same black-eyed pea hairs darted here and there down his belly before disappearing into the grayed waistband of his khakis.

"Saddown, swashbucklers," he said.

But neither me nor Bertha wanted to take our chances with that filthy love seat.

"We just running in, baby brother. We don't need to sit."

"Saddown," he commanded, "or you gone moonwalk the plank on outta here."

We obeyed and perched, close together, on the very edge of that couch. Obviously, he was not having a good day. It seemed like to me that one of us would have offered to help him count out the pills, but me and Bertha and the Mexican woman just sat and watched, caught-up and quiet, as his pained fingers fumbled the fulfillments out one by one.

When I got home, I went straight to the boy's room and pushed the door, not giving a damn what I burst in on. He was on the floor, pumping out push-ups.

I roared at him, "You better get me my GOTDAMN earrings, and you better not make me wait!"

I slammed the door in his astonished face. Out in the hallway, I was glad for both of us that the fulfillment was falling upon me.

DIAMOND

We were coming the back way from the arcade and ended up
stopped at the red light at Yazoo and Issaquena when I saw a
group of men in a shady patch off Yazoo. It was boil-a-nigga
hot outside, but they sat in a semicircle on buckets or milk
crates like they were some sort of council. One, a lanky something, was talking and gesturing wildly with a cigarette stuck
in his fingers. The others were howling at whatever story he
told, and I very much wanted to know what they were talking
about, so I rolled the window down. Heat blasted in, causing
Wonder to look at me. The light changed just as I realized that
I had been staring at but not recognizing my own brother.

"Make a block, Manny. Make a block." I was frantic.

I didn't want Yancey to see me and run off. Wonder had lead-
footed the light, and now we were on the bridge and would not
be able to turn around for three whole streets, and I hoped to
God he would be there when we got back. He was. I told Wonder to pull over and bounded out of the car, calling Yancey's
name.

"Baby girl," he called, and put his arms out.

He tried to say it lightly, but I knew he didn't want me seeing
him. He was the only one of my siblings I could lay my hands
on, so he would have to get over it. I leapt into his arms. I had
not seen him in over a year, and I saw age on him now, his age
plus somebody else's and sickness or drugs. His hair was curly,
overgrown, and his skin was light brown, but he had a smoker's
dark mouth. And still, Cricket and Popeye and Mama were

written all over him, and he was beautiful. I squeezed into his side, burying my wet face into his T-shirt.

"What you crying for, Diamond? Everybody's alive. Everybody's moving on up in the world."

His focus was over my head at Wonder, who was standing on his runner and looking over the top of the truck at me. He raised his chin up and dropped it; slowly Yancey did the same. His friends had stopped talking and were staring at me.

"Damn, Smoke, that's a pretty girl," one of them said.

"Don't I know it?" Yancey said.

"Can we walk?" I asked.

"Of course," he said.

I waved my hand to Wonder, letting him know I was OK, and Yancey and I strolled down the block a bit, out of the earshot of the others. For a while, I just stared, trying to memorize him, storing up for the times that I belonged to nobody and nobody belonged to me.

"Brother, I miss you. I miss everybody."

"Everybody miss you, too," he said, smiling. "You in school still? Set to graduate and everything?"

"Yep, senior year starts in August. I'm going to college, Alcorn maybe. You know you oughta go back to school or something."

"School aint the place for a rough chap like me."

"What are you talking about, Yancey? You were too smart. I know you could pass an ACT with your eyes closed," I said, but his eyes had glazed over like he was done with the subject.

"Say, sis, who's that you're with?"

"They call him Wonderboy. His daddy's a preacher."

Yancey stroked down the sides of his mouth and nodded. "Oh, yeah, they got big money. His ma a feen for them pills, you know."

"I think everybody know but him."

Yancey raised one eyebrow. "Aint no way that chap don't know unless he simple. Well, when you see the mama, tell her I got something for her."

I shrugged because it was what it was. A look in Yancey's face, and we were chuckling together and hugged up like when we were little kids.

"You be careful, hear? The only difference between the niggas in Coon Hill and the ones in the White House is money, so that makes them way more dangerous."

"No, brother, Wonder is the sweetest boy I ever met. He would never hurt nobody."

Yancey looked doubtful, went silent. I nudged him.

"'Member our movie nights?"

He smiled, more inside than outside, then as if he'd just remembered something, he stuck out his wrist and commanded me to look. Ms. Yvonne had gotten a friendship bracelet kit from somewhere and had given it to us. No one had taken to it but me, and I must've made about fifty one summer. Although he said it was stupid at the time, he was wearing it now. I couldn't believe he still had it. I boo-hooed.

"You're going to have to cut that crying shit out, Diamond. So this is what we'll do: give me the number to the house, and I'll call and let you check up on me once in a while."

I dug around my purse for a paper and pen. For some reason, I felt like he would really call me this time. I slipped the twenty Wonderboy had just given me into his pocket. He grabbed my hand.

"Girl, you ought to know not to reach in a man's pocket while he's standing up in his pants."

We started laughing again because we both knew he had just made that up. He hugged me harder this time, and I could feel the extent of his boniness. I hadn't yet been able to figure out what my brother smelled like—like spent matches or the air after a candle was blown out. I liked it, though. He walked me back to the truck and kissed me on the forehead.

"You need something, man?" Wonder asked.

"Naw, I'm good," Yancey said.

Nobody but Wonder knew I wasn't a big believer. We didn't talk much about that kind of stuff anyway. We talked about this life and what it could be, not the so-called next one. Still, that Sunday, I knew the moment they started singing "Thank You, Lord" at the benediction that it was going to get to me. I was sandwiched between Mrs. Kathareen's jutting right hip and for some reason, Mama had her foot hooked around mine. With not one instrument, the whole church sang. Wonderboy and Ivy had picked up the ad-lib. They sang with their heads raised to the sky, their voices weaving around each other's, dipping and arching, and the whole church backed them, not singing as much as vibrating together. I couldn't stop thinking about Yancey, and then I got to wondering about the rest of my siblings, like how Popeye might not even have the same name or may not even really remember us, and suddenly, my eyes were leaking like a faucet. It was all too much. I was embarrassed, wanted to run out of this sanctuary and get to the piece of joint I had in my purse. I tried to get up, but Mrs. Kathareen hemmed me in the pew and dropped her arm around me and forced my head down on her shoulder. Mama held around my waist, and they rocked me between them, a hip holding me in place on one side, a breast on the other. They rocked me while I cried so hard that I couldn't cover my face. I wondered if Wonder could see me, what he might think of my tears.

All the rest of the day got me thinking too much about belief. I had learned early what deserved my trust, and that was things and people that were solid and real. Santa was not solid. Even if he was real, showing up once a year never was the business. God was not solid. He had no shape, no form, nothing but words from a long-ass time ago, and He never showed up regardless, that I knew of. I deduced that He was neither solid, nor real, nor believable.

I watched *The Cosby Show*, not because I loved them so much like everybody else, but because I despised them. I hated Heathcliff most of all, with his dead-eyed, creepy-handed self, and I hated bougie, stuck-up Clair. I hated their *fake*. Nobody ever got smacked in the mouth or sighed umphumphumph when the pipes froze and burst or had braids furry with new growth with beads dangling on them. Clair didn't brace Vanessa's shoulders between her knees to get her parts straight, nor did she ever stand at the sink for a hoe bath. They might seem solid, but they weren't at all real or believable. They could have tried to make it realer. For example, even though the Winfreys had a lot of money like the Huxtables, you could tell they were some fucked-up people. Everybody knew the First Lady couldn't even drive because of DUIs.

Bob Ross was believable, solid, and real.

He had been with me all my life, and you had to believe a person who used the word *thickets* and could sweep a brush of titanium white and Prussian blue across a canvas and make you feel frost when it was ninety degrees outside. I even believed in his fro although Mama told us it was a perm. Best of all, he had the calmest voice I had ever heard come out of a man, and it felt real, not because he was perfect but because you knew that the soft blue shirt with its rolled-up sleeves had the worn-in smell of cigarettes.

Pretty round butt that jutted back behind her. The face wasn't there, but hands down, top three body in the whole school. Plus she had a nasty walk, kind of like a stripper who was a cowboy by day. The type of walk that said exactly what that body could do.

Porky Nelson was one of, if not the best, blocking center in Mississippi 5A. Pound for pound, he was stronger than all of the O-line even at Moss Point or Provine, and he could push a line of defenders back to Texas if you asked him to. He was excitable, though, and Wonderboy knew when Porky's hammy left calf quivered that he was about to false start. Wonderboy would go crazy then; a center aint never got to jump early. It was the reason Porky was no good with the girls. They liked when you took control, *when you had control.* Anyway, Porky was the one who hipped him to the fact that the girl walked like she had good pussy. Any time she was anywhere around the team, the other boys barked out "Hoss," at her backside, even though Porky and Champ them wouldn't know what to do with her if she did a Chinese split on their lap.

When his girl was mad at him, he called this other girl and met her at the New Roxy theater. She wore a stonewashed denim skirt and sleeveless denim shirt that tied at the waist. He got her snacks: chocolate candy, popcorn, and a drink. He didn't get her a hot dog because women shouldn't eat hot dogs in public, and besides, he didn't want to smell it on her later.

As she munched, he stuck his hand in the gap between her shirt, traced her soft skin with his fingers. He could feel when she relaxed, when she transmitted her desire for more. Porky them would be trying to make their move right then, but he knew better. When you treated a hoe like a lady, she would give you anything. After the movie was over, she asked to go to the store, where he bought her a blue floral pillow with arms, a bottle of purple nail polish, and another soda. As they were leaving, she reached to grab his hand, and they began swinging arms, playfully, like kids.

"Do it really hurt when them big ol' boys be hitting you?"

He hurled the stupid pillow into the back seat of the truck and told her to stand where she was.

"Imma show you," he said, and backed up about twenty yards.

He lowered himself into a three-point stance and barreled toward her. She started screaming, but instead of moving out of his way, she held her hands up like she was under arrest. He laughed, a genuine one, and slowed himself down but not enough to keep from driving her backwards. He caught the giggling girl before she could hit the ground. They got in his truck, and he drove them into the alley behind Manna! Restaurant, where heavy petting commenced. He knew this was not her first time at the rodeo, though she tried to play shy. He felt her surrender, though, felt her seize and then surrender to the chastening of this, the holy rod, a Biblical metaphor he'd interpreted himself. When he took her home, he noticed his daddy owned her house; he wondered if she knew. The pillow looked even more ridiculous and gigantic when she got out with it; he offered to carry it for her.

She shook her head. "No, thank you."

"Look, I love you, hear?"

"I love you, too," she said.

4

*I'm just a nobody trying to tell everybody about
somebody who can save anybody.*

FROM THE MINISTER'S DESK

Sabre J. Winfrey

July 2, 2000

MORNING MESSAGE: A Spiritual Clean Sweep

SCRIPTURAL BACKGROUND: "When an unclean spirit goes out of
a man, he goes through dry places, seeking rest, and finding none, he says, 'I will return to my house from which
I came.' And when he comes, he finds it swept and put in
order. Then he goes and takes with him seven other spirits
more wicked than himself, and they enter and dwell there,
and the last state of that man is worse than the first."
Luke 11:24-26 NKJV

SABRE POINTS: Why is there no rest for the unclean spirit?
_____.

How is this scripture reflective of the contagious nature
of hypocrisy?_____
_____

Luke's passage portrays a spirit whose latter state is
worse than the former; how does this relate to John 10:10?
_____
_____

The Book of Ephesians says we must put on the _____
_____.
Why?_____
_____

The Joker slept in the concession stand at Dominion Field when his old lady wouldn't put him up. He was a short, brown man, spare and rangy, and not bad looking at all. A Jody-on-the-spot, a man of many talents—comedy, song and dance, masonry, humane pest extermination, various physical and mental therapeutic ministries, and mob-type shit, among other things. He knew his current situation was a minor setback for a major comeback. Before the military made him who he was at this moment, he had pleasant memories. His sweet mother, whom he had hastened to her grave. Children he had created and loved before he fell off. Women, kinder and prettier than the sometimey one he had now. Often, he preferred the concession stand to his old lady's place anyway. It was far out, past the Jitney Jungle, but it was soundly built, and he had the place to himself. Plus, it was convenient to the trailer park she lived in, so that he could quickly get there should she change her mind. Other than the weekly grass cutting that messed with his sinuses, he had no real issues at all with his spot.

~~~~~

Shining was what Emanuel did, was what he'd always done. Early, he rolled out of bed and dropped to the floor for push-ups to rouse himself fully. Practice started up again in a couple of weeks, and because it was his senior campaign, he needed to be ready to give the Division I biggies courting him one hell of a highlight reel. He jumped from the floor and picked up his student Bible and read the chapters his daddy had outlined for him. Afterwards, he put on a pair of biking shorts and a

T-shirt, brushed his teeth, grabbed one of his daddy's home-made sports drinks, and was off.

In town, there was little traffic, but on the outskirts, rumbling farm machinery had already beat him to work. His daddy owned a great deal of land in the county, had bought it right from under them white boys' noses, and that made him proud. Past the grocery store, he yielded to the right and drove until the stadium loomed ahead. He got out, leaving everything in the truck, not wanting even his keys to slow him down. Striding through the open gate with the soft sun on his face, the bit of breeze, he felt invincible, like the sun and breeze and even the gravel under his feet conspired to make him great.

Once he reached the track, he stretched the kinks out. Sufficiently loose and buoyed by youthful energy, he took an easy jog up the bleachers. When he reached the top where the announcer's booth was, he looked across and saw a man running the bleachers on the away side, moving like a machine and with most excellent form. Emanuel made a shade of his hand and squinted to see better. Who the heck was that? One of them South Panola boys visiting family? Somebody from Ole Miss? He returned to his task, more forcefully now. After three or four trips, he moved toward the track where the stranger was.

It seemed as though he was waiting for Emanuel. Up close, he was darker, more brolic. Without a word, he took off, and Emanuel followed, matched his sprint in speed, power, and determination, like he or Emanuel might be willing to run to the death. He had never met a competitor who was a machine like himself, let alone one who was maybe a little better, he thought, as the stranger's shoulder became his back as he pulled ahead.

Emanuel surged with heart-racing effort and passed him. Finally, the stranger did himself or maybe Emanuel a favor by stopping and falling to the rubber track, heaving and laughing at the same time.

Emanuel reached out to help dude up, and the dude accepted, and then there was this tension, as if this next contest might be arm wrestling. But the dude was pulling him closer, and he was going. He saw and felt lips on his, accepted the tongue crashing about in his mouth. Dude had one hand cradling Emanuel's head; his palm, resting on the stranger's strong, rippled belly, struggled to decide whether to touch or shove. He was stunned by the fiery complexity of how foreign *and* familiar the musky sweat of this other man was. Man! Man! Man! It thunderbolted in Emanuel's head what he was doing; he tore his mouth away as his body revolted. Stuff was splashing out of him, hot bile from his empty stomach. The expulsion brought him to his knees. The stranger put a hand on his back to help him, but Emanuel slung his arm and almost knocked him down.

"Fuck you," he screamed. "Faggot!"

The man disappeared as Emanuel's body coughed up its last, and he collapsed to the gravel, weeping.

~~~~~

On the way to the bathroom, the Joker glanced out and saw two stallion-like men hoofing it around the track. By the time he emerged, the men were holding each other, kissing like it was going out of style. One was vaguely familiar, but the other was someone he had never seen before, which surprised him because the Joker prided himself on knowing just about everybody from Parchman to the Boat. He knew it wasn't none of his business and none of his place to judge, especially with a habit that demanded as much flexibility as his did. Shaking his head and chuckling, he made his way back to the concession stand to prepare to smoke. He was sky-high when he came out again, and he peeped something rather curious. One of the men was gone, but the familiar one was on the ground, crying like his dog and his mama had died on the same day. Right away, he recognized the weeping boy as one of Rev. Winfrey's sons.

"Looka what we have here," he said, rubbing his hands together and chuckling again.

He wanted to tell the boy that the thing he done wasn't nothing. There were a lot of worse things that he could do and be in his lifetime, but the Joker's needs had taught him to recognize an opportunity and strike while the iron was hot. He walked around in front of the bleachers and revealed himself.

"Unhunhunh . . . Imma tell your daddy you messing with them boys."

Cold terror ran through Emanuel; his voice came out almost like a scream. "What you say?"

"You heard me. Imma tell your daddy—unlessen you got some money on you. You got any money?"

The man's smile was sly but not for long. Emanuel lay weeping on that track when Wonderboy, without a word, rose and bowled the man with his weight. The Joker buckled, stunned, into the bottom bleacher. There was a sound like the splinter-ing of ice; he yanked the Joker from where he had landed. The man put his hands up in surrender.

"It aint got to be all this, young blood. I'm sorry. I'm over here fucked-up in the head from malnourishment and shit. I swear I didn't see nothing, son."

"Son? Son?" Emanuel was screaming in earnest now. "I'm not your SON!"

He pulled his arm back like an arrow and drove it again and again into the Joker's face until he fell unconscious. As soon as Wonderboy began to strangle him, the man flashed alive, weaker but with much fight. The Joker's arms were swinging wildly, but Emanuel pressed all the force of his shame, his hate, his fear, his lust onto the Joker's throat, until he gave up the ghost. While attempting to make as little physical contact as possible with the dead man, he dragged the unfortunately col-ored shirt up his torso and loosely knotted it atop his head. He towed the body toward the restroom, remembered:

Sweeping the walkway in front of his daddy's shop, he was twelve and stout, smooth-skinned, and confident. His jeans were pressed, and his button-down shirt was crisp and bright. Ivy and Mack were outside, too, standing with Sergeant Artie Nabors and Bro. Billy Trout, both of whom were on their way in the shop for a haircut. Just then, the Joker approached the group. He wore brownish pants and a brownish undershirt, perhaps the same one that shrouded his dead face, and began to converse with the men as if he, too, was an upstanding citizen.

He was like, "So, yall, while the candy man is eating cheese in the club, and the pimps is wearing white silk after Labor Day,

Nuggy's busy sending flowers to the Princess Di and making her old man mad."

The men and boys were whooping.

"What the hell is this head talking about?" Emanuel had said, swaggering up.

All of the older men whooped again at his bravado.

"This is your brain on drugs, boy," Sergeant Nabors said, pointing. "Now, Joker, you better dance if you want this money."

He held out a five-dollar bill, and for it, the Joker dipped and swirled like James Brown, all the while making various Michael Jackson sounds. Emanuel had seen this man plenty of times, doing these very moves, telling these very jokes, had even laughed at him before. Then, though, the hatred was sour in his mouth, and he had to spit several times as he watched.

~~~~~

On a hunch, Wonderboy drove by the light at Issaquena. Eight o'clock in the morning, and Yancey was there, alone for the moment. He didn't mean to get him involved; he just needed help figuring out what to do.

"You want to make a couple hundred dollars, man?"

"What you need, partner?"

"Helping my daddy haul some stuff. Hop in."

Yancey did. Instead of forcing conversation, he turned the radio on to mask his nervousness. A Jodeci song came on, and he needed to sing along to relax, but he didn't want Yancey to think he was singing to him. He switched to the gospel station.

"Man, can you cut that off?"

When he did, they both noticed his bloody knuckles, his shaking hands. Immediately, one boy looked ahead, while the other looked away. At Dominion Field, Yancey was at first confused; then, Emanuel gestured for him to exit the truck and follow. The bathroom where he'd stashed the Joker smelled ferocious.

"Fuck, man. What the fuck happened out here?"

Blood smudged the dirt-stained floor. In the third stall, the Joker's body had flopped backwards on the grimy toilet. The shirt tied around the man's head had fallen loose. Yancey fished around for his cigarettes, found a match, and lit up. He inhaled and blew the smoke up his nose.

"I don't know what to do with him."

"Shit, nigga, leave him there."

"If we leave him here, somebody gone find him."

"Did you do this? Why you do this? Joker wasn't no bad guy."

"Tell me what to do with him, Yancey."

The older boy sighed. "Did you check his pockets?"

"I doubt crackheads carry ID."

But Wonderboy took the advice and patted him down anyway, carefully just in case there were needles. He found no ID or money but a tiny, curled snip of sandwich bag and a browned and curled notebook, every page filled with unsteady writing. On the first was printed the name Midas T. Benny. Emanuel stuck the notebook under his armpit and gave the rocks in the snip of bag to Yancey. Yancey's idea was to drop the Joker in Moon Lake, and it seemed like a good idea to Emanuel, plus he already had tarp. So he pulled his truck as close to the restroom as possible; then the boys rolled the Joker up in it and carried him out like a log. The trip to Moon Lake was long and quiet. When finally they got there, they realized they would have no way to hold the Joker down in the water, so they ended up driving into a woodsy area not too far away that didn't entertain much traffic until deer season rolled around.

They toted the body, moving quickly but careful not to trip over a root or step on a snake. Light, dark, light, dark, cool brown trees, a resting place for the Joker. Ready to be done with it all, Wonderboy dropped the Joker's feet in the first secluded-looking spot, but Yancey laid his head down carefully and with respect, considering under the tarp, the man's face looked like meatloaf. By nine, Yancey was sweeping the last of the bleach into the drainage hole, and it smelled better than it ever had in there.

As Emanuel headed home, the morning's events dipped and swelled and swirled themselves in his head. At one point, his mind went too far, to where he was pulled down to the warm gravel and . . . and what? What would have happened next? He imagined doing to the guy what he had done to the Joker. The guy was big, but Wonderboy could have taken him. It troubled him—whatever thing he had emitted that caused the man to try him. He would never have attempted that with his father or brother Mack, definitely not Mack. Emanuel parked his truck in the alley, went in the back door, and snuck up the stairs. He was thankful neither of his parents intercepted him; he didn't know what he'd do if they had. Part of him thought he would just blurt out a confession; part of him thought he'd cry.

Never in a million years would he have thought he'd be on some faggotry. But he had indeed stood shirtless with another man's sweat in his mouth, mingled with his own, kissing him. Even though he had to have seen the guy's face, try as he might, he couldn't recall it, and that made the memories even more frightening. No face meant it could be filled in with any face—like Porky's or Demarcus's or Champ's.

"Good run," the stranger said, reaching out.

Wonderboy had taken the hand, just for dap, of course, and the stranger pulled him forward, catching him off guard. He was surprised more by the intensity of his response than the response itself, the fact that for a time, he had fully committed himself to kissing this man. The situation brought up even more conflicting issues: like the locker rooms and fanny slaps and chest bumps he'd participated in most of his life. And then this: Had the man seen him, baited, raced, and dapped him, all to seduce him? That would mean he had been the bitch! And then the Joker came up, trying to bend him over again. The chap, as Diamond would say, sealed his own fate when he called Wonderboy *son*. Did he look like he could be the son of a crackhead? Despite his turmoil, the satisfying thud the Joker made when he hit the ground brought him a bit of joy.

"It aint got to be all this," the man had said.

But you couldn't un-ring a bell, nor could you expect to pull back a train with a rope. Emanuel ripped off his clothes and jumped in a cloudy, hellish shower. He had let a man kiss his mouth, had maybe kissed that man back, and that meant he was a faggot, a sissy, a *punk*. Showering made him think of Parchman, which was full of punks. Yancey could be somewhere right now ratting him out. He would kill Yancey before he went to jail, and he would kill himself. Forcing his fears out of his head, he got out of the shower and gargled with strong mouthwash as long as he could stand it. He saw to his tattered knuckles. He dried himself, put on a pair of boxers, and fell across his bed into a fitful sleep. Three Jokers peered down at him from different angles, meaty faces dangling so close. An eyeless man chased him, bearing the hugest, most relentless erection imaginable, a man who chased without tiring. And the most terrifying of all, the silhouette of a man who beckoned him to the backyard with a leather strap.

~~~~~

His mother was a bird, pecking and fluttering in and out of the room as he slept.

"Oh, Emanuel," she chirped.

Pressed her cool hand to his forehead and hmmphed like a doctor with a challenge. She returned with water and a bowl of soup. When she tried to rustle him up to eat, he had to stop himself from swatting her. At least she woke him up before certain events could come together in his nightmares.

~~~~~

Before Yancey got to his speedball, Diamond was on his mind. He saw her like he saw her the other day: lanky body, hair cloud, and nails, still bitten-down just like Popeye's. Then his mind stuck on his only brother, stocky and stubborn, wherever he might be, and then Cricket, his best and first friend. Skinny Cricket, who had gotten away from Dominion and cut him and Diamond off like a bad habit. The dirty money burned a hole in his pocket: all this for less than two hours of work, part of that being just riding. And now it was raining, so anything they might have left out there would be soaked, destroyed.

He found his product, balled up in a receipt for the Xpress Mart, and prepared his hit. Cold, crystal light was taking over his brain, a cold, crystal light and a deep inner peace. He loved the peace, but maybe he loved the chase, too. The chase made him noble, made him accomplished. Every day he made a goal, and every day he got it done. He was alright. Everybody was alive and moving up in the world. So why had he been worried about Diamond again?

DIAMOND

Mrs. Kathareen once said red was for love, and that if I loved somebody to burn a red candle for them. Well, she wasn't actually talking to me; I had overheard her telling Maggie and figured if anybody knew about love, it would be her. So as soon as Wonder asked if he could come over, the plaintive, husky sound of his voice told me everything. I took my candle from where I had hidden it, set it on top of my dresser, and lit it, concentrating fiercely on what I wanted: and that was for us to be bound. Now the tiny flame shivered but withstood the breeze from the box fan in the window. We were in my daybed, and his hand was between my legs, causing this thrumming that was maybe the same as how his instruments felt when being played.

"I want to make sure you love me," he told me.

I was caressing his shoulders, arms, his back. "Don't hurt me."

He smelled like outside, the rain, and he felt like the thunder. Afterwards, I lay in his arms, aching sweetly, watching the moonbeams flash through the fan blades. It could have been a streetlight, but wouldn't a streetlight rather be a moonbeam? It was just that kind of night. Finally, the thunder began, and all of it, the dark, the pounding rain, the tiny-flickering candlelight, and especially us, was so beautiful my chest might have cracked and bled out had his hand not held it together.

"I need to know you will love me forever . . . Whatever happens, whatever you hear, whatever . . . ," he said.

"You got that," I said. "What's wrong?"

He shook his head, but I felt his lashes shivering under my palm and his tears shivering under that. My body went faint at his mysterious pain. Did he know he couldn't cry without me? Before I could explain, he jumped out of bed. A splash of uninvited light blotted the small and mighty candle, drowning the magic that was. As I saw him picking up his clothes.

"Where are you going? She won't be home until seven. Please don't go."

"I have to," he said.

"At least wait until morning."

But he didn't.

I woke the next morning, all tender, loose, and chill-bumped. Squeezed my legs to see if I could reclaim the sensations from the night before. I quickly realized I didn't have to; we could do what we had done again and again and in all types of ways. Now that we had taken this step together, was he as changed as I was? A dreaminess accompanied me all morning, and I know I did things, regular things like eating and sweeping and watching TV, but in reality, I probably couldn't have told you my name if you asked. By late afternoon, I felt odd that he hadn't called, so we could discuss this new phase of our relationship, so I called him, but his line rang unanswered. Over the next couple of hours, I called at least ten times, and then I tried the house phone, but it, too, rang unanswered. The next day was Saturday, and there was no word from him. On Sunday, he was not at church; Rev got in the pulpit and mentioned Wonder was visiting Ole Miss, something he hadn't told me at all. I was sick to my stomach.

PRISCILLA

For the Fourth of July, I washed and dried four Cornish hens, buttered and seasoned them, and stuffed them with garlic, onions, and green pepper. I set them into the roasting dish and poured in a quart of chicken broth. I made the Russian potato salad from a recipe I'd seen in the Summer Sparkle edition of *Southern Living*. The corn I shucked and boiled. The yeast rolls, purchased from Eliza Walker School, I baked and buttered. I had put this delicious meal on the table, and Ivy was eating like it was going out of style, but Emanuel was moving his food around his plate. I was heartened to think that his conscience was bothering him for disrespecting me and this house.

"You OK, boy?" Rev asked him.

"Yessir," Emanuel said, and took the smallest bite of potato salad.

"Deacon McGlown asked me again if yall wanted to play for Shell's wedding in December. I told him I'd see since I know things are going to be hectic around that time. You got the Blue/Gray game and all sorts of recruiting stuff happening."

"I'm down," Ivy said. "I can probably get Mack if you can't do it, Manny."

"Cool," said Emanuel. "Dad, will you edge me up before you leave?"

"I was wondering how long you were going to walk around with that hair crawling down your neck with your daddy being the slickest barber this side of glory. You make me shame, boy." Rev laughed.

Emanuel cleared his throat, abruptly got up, and left the dining room. I heard him scraping his plate into the trash and putting it in the sink.

"What's wrong with him?" Ivy said.

"He's a star. That's a tough row to hoe, too," Rev said.

Rev got up and slid his plate in my direction.

"Wrap this up for me, Cilla. I gotta go down to the station for a little while."

I turned to glare at him. "What's needed down at the station, Sabre, today on a holiday?"

"Yeah, Imma get on out of here, too," Ivy added on.

"You just got here, baby."

"I have a lil friend I'm hanging out with tonight. I just wanted to come eat good and kiss my favorite girl."

I smiled at him. "You should've brought her."

"Ma, aint nobody doing all that these days. You can meet her if I think I might marry her, OK?"

He was right, and I don't know why I said otherwise. It was none of my business what my sons did with these fast-tail girls.

Later on into the evening, Sabre was still out. I talked to my sister for a while, and then I noticed just how quiet the house was. Manny hadn't left that room since he left the table, and I hoped to God he was sleeping—because what else could he be doing so quietly? It crossed my mind that just because you birthed somebody didn't mean you knew them. My weird boys, Trey and Moshe, were smart as whips and had never given me a whiff of trouble. They were closer to each other than any people I knew. Mack was my buck boy; he could be gruff, but he was a sweetie if he let you get close. Ivy, the most sensitive of my boys, was good at drawing and putting things together. I had thought Emanuel was the best of them, of us.

Sick and tired of all this thinking, I decided to grab me a little drink and wind down for bed early. I turned on the radio and sat at the vanity to wrap my hair. I guess the Lord said otherwise because Betty Sykes and the Dundee Battle Axes came on singing "Agape." Betty's anointing brought the Spirit flush on me, and my hands went up in the air, right where I sat. My eyes closed, and the tears rained down.

"ThankyouthankyouLordIwanttothankyou," I called.

A knock on the door interrupted my praise, and I fluttered

my lids open just enough to see Emanuel in the door watching me. Betty's singing, however, strengthened my resolve to rebuke the drop of Satan that had taken up residence in the body of my son.

"Precious Jesus, free him," I whispered, closing my eyes again. "Free him. Free him. Make whatever it is turn my boy loose."

When I opened my eyes, he was gone, but my earrings were there on the vanity. And you know what, I felt guilty for some reason. That almost-man, my mind saw as six years old again, staring at a dying dog. I had scooped him up, held him to my heart, patted his back to comfort him. Then I knew precisely everything about him, all he could want and need as well as how to solve those wants and needs. Now I didn't even want to know what I didn't know about him.

"Ma," he'd called out with the cruel sound of pain and bewilderment.

I looked around, startled, trying without success to establish whether I'd heard the sound in my ear, my mind, or my heart. A lump rose in my throat I couldn't swallow over.

DIAMOND

The hours ticked on without a word from Wonderboy. By the sixth day, I was beginning to think I was a complete fool. For laying with him, for loving him, for always finding reasons to hope shit was gone go right in my life for once. I found myself overwhelmed by the same trembly raw uncertainty I had when the people came and got us out of the Sunflower. Would I always be straddling my past and present? Was that the reason I could never clearly see a future? Forreal, it wasn't like I wasn't aware things like this happened. All the time you heard boys say stuff like "hit it and quit it." I was just surprised at *him*. I had always seen him as better than the other boys, quieter and more mature. Also because he didn't have to try to trick someone out of their draws when anybody would gladly give him some.

The whole Fourth of July was a bust for me. By noon, I was already sick of the kids, the fireworks, and the stank of burnt meat. I was sick of Maggie's puzzled stares and concern. She had the whole week off, and I wanted nothing more than for her to go away. I knew I should be ashamed; I couldn't even imagine where I'd be without her. She was a poor widow who had brought me into her home and family, had fish fries and car washes, and begged the church for help adopting me. And here I was, ungrateful, only able to focus on the people who had abandoned me. After dinner, I slipped into my room, turned on my television, and held myself in my arms, rocking, but I couldn't be soothed, at least not by me. The door opened, and there Maggie stood.

"Awww, what's wrong, baby girl?"

"I keep thinking about my mama. It's almost her birthday," I said, which wasn't entirely a lie.

"Do you want to talk about it?"

"Sometimes I think God just don't like me."

"God loves everybody, Diamond, especially you," she said.

But, of course, it sounded fake as hell to me, like precisely what someone would think they should say in a situation like this.

"Well, He sure got a hell of a way of showing it," I said.

Maggie said, "God's ways is mysterious to us piddly humans. All we need is to know it's gone be OK because He's working in our favor."

I struggled not to roll my eyes at her answer. I hugged her tighter because a body was a body, and although it wasn't the one I wanted to be embracing, it meant I was not alone.

"You want to go to the riverfront for the fireworks?"

"I'm good, Mama," I said. "I promise. Anybody can get down sometimes."

I was hoping that would be enough for her, but it wasn't.

She said quietly, "What about Rev's boy?"

"We're taking it slow," I said.

"I was going to say you needed to lay off him anyway. You're too young for a serious relationship. You've stopped doing the stuff you used to like. You don't go to the library. Or bake. Or skate. It's not healthy."

"That has nothing to do with him. I just, I just—" But I couldn't find a lie.

"Well, some young man called and asked for you while I was on the phone, but he wouldn't say who he was."

Yancey, I thought, and flew off the bed and into the living room where the nearest extension was and checked the caller ID, but the number was from a pay phone. Maggie peeked into the room.

"It could have been my brother. I saw him the other day and gave him the number."

"Oh, good for you, baby," she said. "I'm sure he'll call back."

As soon as she left the room, I picked up the phone again and carefully plugged in *67, so the number would show up as private. The Winfreys' phone rang twice before the First Lady answered. I said nothing, breathed quietly, hoping to hear him in the background.

"Stop calling here, whoever this is," she hissed.

I slammed down the phone in her face. I didn't realize how much I hated her flimsy voice. I plopped on the sofa and turned on the television; Maggie joined me but kept dozing off in front of the movie we started. She left for bed finally, and relieved, I wandered out to the porch. Half past ten and most of the fireworks in the neighborhood had stopped, but miles away, the ones at the river were still in full swing. The moon hung fake, white, and faraway in a low, ugly charcoal sky. My skin was crawling under my nightgown. I went inside to keep it from stripping away from my weak bones and flying off into the lonesome sky.

In my bedroom, I concentrated on things that would keep me sad. The day I almost saw Cricket was the first thing I thought of, and it definitely did the trick. I was in the sixth grade, and me and Genecia Murray got to be fast friends. Genecia was kin to Cricket's stepmother, and she took a whipping for getting me the number. But she told me it was worth it because she couldn't imagine not being able to talk to her big sister. And I decided then to love her forever. Wherever she is, I have love for her still. Anyway, I got permission and called the same night. Cricket answered the phone; she was a big girl, in the ninth grade. We cried a little. I told her she sounded the same; she told me I did not.

Maggie and the stepmother set up a meeting at the Shoney's on Winchester for that next weekend. Cheryl, Maggie's oldest daughter, drove us because Maggie hated driving in Memphis, and she brought along her baby, Gigi. Gigi was three and happy because she was going to have pancakes, and it wasn't even breakfast time. I rushed everybody out of the house that morning, and we ended up arriving fifteen minutes early. We sat at the very first table with me facing the door; I insisted on being the first person Cricket saw when she came in. But we waited and waited, and they never arrived, and when we called, the number had been changed.

"I told you not to trust them saditty-ass people, Mama," Cheryl said as we pulled off without ordering. "They think they're too good for everybody!"

Gigi had to settle for a corn dog from the convenience store on the way out; when she bit it, she declared it cornbread and heaved herself into a tantrum. Maggie rocked the baby, and Cheryl crawled into the back seat and held me.

"Never again." She shook her finger. "Never!"

She had been so fierce that day—the embrace she gave me was crushing and sweet. I needed her fire right at that moment because the wind had shonuff been knocked out of me.

8-000706

Emanuel, who had been holding his secret for over a week, went into his mother's bedroom to say, *Ma, I messed up*, but he couldn't bring himself to say the words. For one, the radio was blasting, and his mother was half-dressed and so-called full of the Spirit, so now he wanted to crush her. He shook his head to erase this train of thought. Stuff like this would get him sent straight to Whitfield, which he heard was as bad as, if not worse, than Parchman. Fortunately, his mother had not opened her eyes; he set her earrings down and returned to his room.

He sat on his bed and thought on the aftermath. Yancey kept saying the Joker wasn't no bad guy. How the hell wasn't a crackhead a bad guy? It made him think of the Easter pageant one year. Moshe was Jesus, the best they ever had, most people said. All Emanuel knew was that they had had to perform the Easter pageant four times that year instead of three because of him. Trey was Judas, and Mack was Peter. Ivy and himself were in the children's choir, watching their big brothers and the other boys in robes on the long, rugged bench that had been tacked together by Brother McMillian.

"One of you will betray me," Moshe said with quiet resolution.

The disciples stopped serving themselves dinner rolls and looked at Jesus in shock. Just then, Trey stuck his hand in the bowl at the same time as Moshe, and the lights went dim except for a spotlight on Trey, and he boomed out his solo, "Is It I, Lord? Is It Me?" like his name was Paul Robeson. When he was done, there was not a dry eye in the house. The whole time, Emanuel couldn't help but feel sorry for Judas and his situation. He was the most hated person in the Bible, and the only reason he did what he did to Jesus was because somebody had to do it. That day had been coming since the dawn of time, so why was he hated just for serving his purpose? Was that not honorable? And Trey was singing with the rightful emotion associated with the act of betraying a gentle, perfect man who only came to heal and save.

The Joker wasn't innocent, thought Emanuel; he definitely wasn't innocent. The man was trying to extort him! And how could he allow a man to hold power over him? He recalled something Shaka Zulu's mother said in the miniseries—well, first he remembered Shaka, whose fierce fitness reminded him of his father—but anyway, Shaka's mother advised him never to leave an enemy behind. It would only be a matter of time before the Joker told somebody, and it would be like when everybody in school was saying his mother was in the grocery store butt naked. Or worse, when Champ them made Monte Parham drop out because somebody said somebody said he was junk-watching in the locker room.

Emanuel went down on his knees, bowed his head, and clasped his hands, shuddering at a flashback of them pressing the life out of a man. And although he said his prayers every night and had often led his teammates and peers in prayer, he could find neither the right words nor the right approach. He thought about how his daddy might pray if he were in this position, but that, too, was fruitless, so he got off his knees and returned to his bed. Before long, he was dreaming again: this time, the stranger on the track had put the Joker back together. Rubbery scars crisscrossed the new face, and his new smile was bigger, more jokerly. Emanuel jolted from sleep with a sound like a yelp and a grimace. He was overaware of himself in that moment: his jagged, open-mouthed breathing, the rush-rush of blood in his ears, and it felt almost exactly like he was in a big game or right when he'd excelled at something. Instead of glory, though, he felt fear, an emotion he had grown highly unfamiliar with and adverse to. He lay himself down gingerly, willed his body to calm.

The deed was done, he told himself, and it was what it was. He had done everything right afterwards, too: they had cleaned the bathroom and washed and detailed his truck. So, why was he still so worried? Why the fuck had he gone to get Yancey in the first place? He could have done all that stuff on his own . . . but Yancey had thought of the bleach and had spotted the Joker's red skullcap on the bleachers. He guessed Yancey had enough sense not to say nothing to nobody; he'd be in trouble, too. Still, he felt he couldn't be too sure because they had never discussed it during the whole field trip.

He jumped out of bed and into basketball shorts and a T-shirt. He slipped on a pair of slides and got his keys. He had to find Yancey, had to make sure. *I don't want to have to kill you, partner*, he would say, *but I will*. Yancey was no more than 130 pounds stretched across five feet, ten inches—he could mangle him even worse than the Joker. Yep, he had to find Yancey, and maybe he would use Diamond for insurance. Since the

Reaping Season had been in full swing, the city curfew shut everything for teens down at eleven. Still, it was summertime, and older and younger folk were still out and about in pockets. He didn't see Yancey around, not on Issaquena or any of the other spots a dude like him might hang out. He did find Caticia Wooten, walking near Fourth and Howard, and changed his mission. A year ahead of him, she hadn't graduated with her class in May. Still, he was surprised to see her out because she had been sort of quiet. He drove up to her, rolled down the window.

"I need somebody to hang out with," he said.

"Don't you go with that girl, Diamond?"

"You could go with me, too," he said.

His smile made her comfortable, and she slid, smiling, into the passenger seat. Small and cocoa brown, she wore a faded blue shirt with strawberries on it and a denim skirt. She was making her grape Bubble Yum sound like a Thanksgiving meal. He asked her for a piece, and patiently, he waited as she reached in her small pocketbook for it. He opened his mouth for her to feed it to him. The purple sweetness of the gum jolted his taste buds; his chewing sounds filled up his ears.

"What you doing out here this late, Tish? You hoeing?" His question rattled her, he could tell. "Who would have known that slow-ass Caticia Wooten would be hoeing?"

"Your mama's slow," she said, pointing to her hip.

He chuckled, long and loud, to fill the car. "Caticia Wooten, I didn't know you were funny, too."

She grabbed the car handle as if to let herself out, but the door was locked. Gregory Abbott was on the radio, singing smoothly about wanting to shake somebody down. The song seemed perfect for the occasion; he sang along. He would shake her down alright. From the corner of his eye, he saw her relax a bit, lulled by his voice. Abruptly, he shut off the radio, finishing the note.

"I killed my dog," he said.

He knew this was what he needed to gain his power back.

"Um, whet?"

Her gum went back to popping. He hated these hoodrat chicks.

"I killed him because he was dumb, and he kept making my daddy mad. So I strung him up on the fence and choked him and watched his eyes bug out. I didn't want him anymore."

The girl looked like she was in a trance.

"You crazy, boy," she said.

"I know."

That night, for the first in many, there were no dreams and no fears to jerk him awake.

5

I'm just a nobody trying to tell everybody about somebody who can save anybody.

FROM THE MINISTER'S DESK
Sabre J. Winfrey

July 9, 2000

MORNING MESSAGE: A Reflection Is More Than Skin-Deep

SCRIPTURAL BACKGROUND: "As in water face reflects face, so a man's heart reveals the man. Hell and Destruction are never full; so the eyes of man are never satisfied. The refining pot is for silver and the furnace for gold, and a man is valued by what others say of him. Though you grind a fool in a mortar with a pestle along with crushed grain, yet his foolishness will not depart from him." Proverbs 27:19-22 NKJV

SABRE POINTS: These Proverbs speak to the soul _____ of a man.

How can the Christian ensure he or she measures up to God's standards?_____

_____

How is our behavior a reflection of and reflected in our consumption and overconsumption (e.g., TV, food, gossip)? Why is contentment a necessity to Godly living?

_____

_____

What is the danger of the live-and-let-live mentality? How is this evident in our community?_____

_____

Jimmy Wooten had worked a double shift as a slot attendant at the Lady Liberty Casino in Robinsonville. It wasn't a difficult job, but fourteen hours of doing anything would make anybody feel as worn out and frustrated as he did. Parking his Plymouth in front of his neat, pleasant Brickyard home and loosening the bow tie improved his mood. He grabbed his bag and his fanny pack and got out of the car. It was after four, and even though it was a little early still, today was his Friday, so he cracked open his Old Milwaukee on the way to sweep the mailbox with his hand. Finding it empty, he stuck his key in the lock and pushed the front door open. His eyes had to adjust from the bright afternoon sunshine to the dimness of the room; he turned on the light, opened the blinds, and looked around. The disheveled living room re-ticked him off. His wife, Marsha, had left for work at 6:45 this morning, and these girls hadn't half cleaned up.

"Why is it so dark in here? Where are the girls, Reggie?"

The boy, who was eight, made a half-hearted shrug. Jimmy took a long swig of his beer and knuckled his son's head on his way to his daughters' bedroom. He shook the knob, but it was locked. They knew not to lock their bedroom door.

"Open this damn door. What's going on in there?"

Jimmy heard them whispering and shifting, but the door remained closed. He shouldered it just a little, just enough to let them know that he would break it open momentarily. Asia, the younger girl, opened up. Jimmy looked at her and then at Caticia curled up under the covers in a ball so small he could barely see her.

"What's wrong?" he asked.

"She been like this all day," said Asia.

"Get up, Caticia," he said.

He had to peel his baby girl out of the bed. When he looked at the cluster of tooth prints on the ball of her cheek, he began to weep.

"Who did this? Who did this to you, baby?"

———

At the front door of the Winfreys, Jimmy was nervous, and he could tell Caticia was, too. He was still clad in his work cummerbund and slacks, and Caticia was wearing yesterday with some wind suit pants he made her put on. He felt shabby against the grand stone house, with its manicured lawn, the flowers that looked too bright to be real. Despite his mission here, Jimmy was taken aback by the sultry eyes and plush lips of the Reverend's wife and had to catch his bearing to keep his voice from trembling.

"Ma'am, my name is Jimmy Wooten, and I need to speak to the pastor," he said.

"Reverend Winfrey is not in at the moment, but I am Mrs. Winfrey. Can I assist you in some way?"

The man pulled the girl over the threshold, and Priscilla shut the door. She invited them to sit in the living room, but Jimmy refused for the both of them.

"Where is that boy?"

"Pardon me?"

"Your boy, your son—he assaulted her. Look at her face. I just want you to see what your crazy nigger done before we go to the police station."

The woman's face bore no identifiable emotion; Jimmy thought she ought to be on the boat playing the poker tournament. She pointed toward the left window.

"Chief Nabors is two doors down on the other side of the street. Go to the door under the carport. But, sir, I hope you have evidence to back up these libelous claims when you go down there."

"Libelous, fribelous—I'd kill the motherfucker myself if I didn't have a family to feed, but come hell or high water, he's going to jail."

"Mr. Wooten, I have to ask you to modulate your tone and respect my Godly home."

Jimmy pushed and turned the girl, revealing a bruise that bloomed from her shoulder to her elbow.

"This Godly to you?"

The woman gasped and put her hand on her chest. "Mercy, child, what happened to you?"

Suddenly, everyone turned around. Emanuel was coming down the stairs, looking broad and dazzling in a red tracksuit. Jimmy's face showed awe and then recognition and anger. He almost lunged—the nerve of this motherfucker, to treat his baby like she meant nothing to nobody.

"Hey, Tish," Wonder said, raising his hand to wave.

It irritated Jimmy even more that this boy had spoken her name in this way, like they were familiar. His mother took him by the hand.

The woman said, "Do you know this young lady, son? Her father seems to think you hurt her."

The boy's smooth face was shocked.

"What? She asked me for a ride home last night, and as soon as she got in the car, she told me she would sell me some for seventy-five dollars. I told her I didn't roll like that, and she told me to drop her off in front of a house on Cherry Street. Somebody else did that."

"What?" Jimmy Wooten lurched.

"He lying, Daddy!" were Caticia's first words.

"Tish, I'm lying?"

Jimmy had worked full-time hours since he was fourteen years old. Marsha worked hard as hell, too. Asia was in the honors classes, and Reggie was doing sixth-grade math in the third grade, and here Caticia was eighteen gotdamn years old, and all he and his wife had asked her to do was to get a damn GED and a trade. He had always told his daughter she was pretty. And he hadn't been like his kinfolks who thought you oughta raise kids without compassion, like they'd been raised; he hugged his kids all the time, especially his daughters. Could she have really been out here selling herself under his nose? The blood in Jimmy's head was bubbling like soup about to boil over. He realized all at once that he had been sweating and that everybody was looking at him crazy. Had he been talking out loud?

"I'm sorry I barged in over here like this," he said with a voice that croaked. "Me and my girl got some talking to do."

"Jimmy," the Reverend's wife said, "can I tell you that God heals? Can I tell you that He saves and heals? Can I tell you that He saves and heals and chastens? Are you and your family in the church, sir?"

The Wooten family already belonged to Macedonia Baptist, and although Jimmy wasn't a churchy man, he remembered hearing their boys singing at a revival back in '93 and having been moved to tears at their rendition of his mother's favorite hymn: "Somewhere to Lay My Head." He had seen this boy hurdle linebackers into the end zone on numerous Friday nights. He jammed to WDOZ early mornings on his way to work. He didn't want a row with these people; they were everywhere. He didn't want his family's name dragged because whether she'd done what he'd said or not, all it took was the idea to get out and about to ruin their name.

Jimmy sighed. He decided that they would tell her mama that she had gotten to fighting, and even though that would still probably earn her a vigorous ass whipping, Marsha would kill this girl if she got a whiff of this other shit. Maybe he would kill this asshole—Wonderboy, they called him—Mr. Football—Mr. El DeBarge. Jimmy was a well-used forty, and he knew he didn't want to tussle with this corn-fed nigger; he would have to shoot him.

"Can I pray for you?" the Reverend's wife asked, pulling a bottle of holy oil out of thin air, it seemed to Jimmy and his bewildered girl.

PRISCILLA

After the Wootens left, I stood outside the front door, staring out at the space where their car had been. Laser imprinted in my mind was the small, brown, marred face of that girl. I gripped the small medicine bottle of holy oil, not wanting to go back inside. In fact, I wanted to be far, far away from there and free, like my friend Billie Jean, who divorced her husband when we were in our twenties and never looked back, never even thought about remarrying or having some damn children. She was always inviting me to go to this country or that with her, and I never did. I decided that if I got through this situation, I would start going with her, and I might not come back. I went into my house and closed the door quietly; the boy waited for me in the living room. I took a deep breath but forgot to exhale.

"Did you do those things to her?"

I almost phrased it differently, like, *I know you didn't do those things to her*, but I thought better of that. His face bore a hint of amusement, which I hoped I was imagining.

"Do you think I did it?"

"Before I would have said no, none of my sons were capable of brutality, but now, I really don't know."

"Mama, you know."

I sighed. "I have to call your father. I do not want you to leave this house."

"I'm going to lift weights," he said, calling my bluff. "I will be back when he gets home, and I will accept my punishment then. Oh, and Mama, that's not all I have to tell you."

He was gone and I let out my pent-up breath. Instead of calling Sabre, I took a couple of nerve pills and let myself into Emanuel's bedroom. The room was neat as a pin. Trophies and plaques for this and that glittered all over his bureau and in the case his daddy got built for him. The twins were tidy, but Emanuel was fastidious. I almost didn't want to touch anything, but I needed to figure out what he had going on, or he'd end up like them white boys that shot up that school. Beside the bed on his nightstand were his student Bible and a small, curled, weather-beaten notebook. I opened it, and on the first page, a name was printed, in tight-fisted penmanship, a title: Tales of a Joker, by Midas T. Benny. What in the world was this boy doing with Tyrone Benny's notebook?

I opened the top drawer in his nightstand, found nothing unusual. In the bottom drawer was a box of newspaper clippings of his achievements, and under it a locked box. I removed it, picked the lock, and found sealed envelopes, eight of them, each labeled and numbered in Emanuel's small, neat handwriting. I picked out one and saw its middle bulged, wasn't slim and flat like an envelope should be. I squeezed it and knew there was something fabric on the inside, something soft. Without opening a single one, I replaced them, all the while blocking my mind's attempts to decipher the contents. This boy feral, I thought, wild. And though I felt bad for thinking it, I also couldn't help but know that whatever he'd done, they'd manage to blame me. They always blamed the mother.

DIAMOND

July 6, I woke, prepared to do more faking the funk. I cooked pancakes and cheese eggs, cleaned the kitchen, and got dressed. On a whim, I laced on my skates and cruised the neighborhood, ignoring boys and dodging the box Chevys that sped through here all the time. And even though I did it as a show for Maggie, as I rounded the corner toward home, I realized I actually did feel better. I could have done a hundred more blocks, but I came home at a good time, right as Maggie was taking out the trash. I removed my skates and gave her a hug and a kiss. Later, the heat in the tub made me think too much of him and how we had felt together, and I felt sad again. On top of it all, I realized I had lost the wonderful earrings he'd given me, too. It was all bad.

The next evening, when Maggie left to go out with Dennis, I threw on some sweats and a tank top, a pair of slip-on canvas shoes. I walked out of the house, not knowing whether I intended to go find Wonder or just get some air. I left the yard, jogged a block, and then ran like crazy. I kept running until I came to Roosevelt Street, where there was the stark, fresh smell of somebody washing clothes to stop me in my tracks. It triggered a full-blown vision of my mama, so beautiful and complex and real, that I stopped running to put my arms around her, and I felt her arms around me. I choked back happy sobs. This was a good sign. I was only back in the house a couple of minutes when an unknown number rang our line. I snatched the phone up.

"Yancey?"

"Emanuel," he said.

I froze, as if I'd heard a ghost, then slammed the phone down. Minutes later, there were knocks on the door, and he stood in our threshold staring down at me.

"You look sick," he said.

"You look sick yourself."

"I am," he said. "I really am."

I was happy to see him there in the flesh, relieved, too, like he had thrown me off the ship but then tossed me a life jacket. I invited him to sit down, but he wouldn't.

"I'm in trouble," he said.

"What's wrong? What kind of trouble?" My hand was on my chest, my heart beating fast underneath it.

"Big trouble."

"What happened? What did you do?" I was glad there was an explanation for him being MIA, but it sucked that it was something terrible that caused it.

"You would hate me if I told you."

"Baby, there is *nothing* you can do to make me hate you. *Nothing.*"

But he shook his head. "I just came here because I'm leaving town, and I wanted to tell you I loved you. I didn't want to just disappear on you."

His words sent me reeling. "*What? When?* Where are you going?"

"I don't know. I'll figure it out when I'm on the road."

"Oh my God, Wonder. What the hell? You got me so gone over here. This is crazy."

He shrugged.

"Come on, baby. Let's talk about this. You can't just leave."

I tried to pull him toward the couch, wanting to comfort him and to comfort myself in his arms. He resisted my efforts, unmovable like that tree we sang about in church. Which made me think of some myth I had read about the lovers who instead of dying became intertwined trees. We would be like those lovers.

"If I asked you to go with me, would you?"

"Yes," I said.

"Pack some stuff then."

I ran into my room, yanked my duffel bag out of my closet, and pitched in various items. To be honest, I didn't even care what I packed. I didn't care what I looked like. All I knew was that Emanuel was in trouble, and I couldn't let him deal with it alone. If he was running away, we were running away, and wherever we went, we'd be there together. As we left the house, I was nervous, thinking of what Maggie's reaction would be when she realized I was gone. I still didn't let that keep me from buckling myself in.

"Oh, maybe we can cross the bridge to Helena and get married."

"Slow down, lil mama."

He said this and laughed, revving us off the curb. A left turn onto Milne Street, we zoomed past the gigantic sanctuary and stopped at the Xpress Mart to fill the tank. On the way out of town, all the lights went green for us, and like that, we were on our way south on 49, not toward Arkansas, but out of Dominion nonetheless.

"You can't get us there no faster doing that," he said, grinning.

I glanced down and saw that I had been pressing my foot on an imaginary gas pedal. If you asked me though, I was powering this car, if not with my foot, with my joy. I threw my head back and watched the stars flash over the moonroof, astonished at how they twinkled at us. I felt like a great big hallelujah, or maybe a shout, even deeper than how it felt when I smelled the fresh laundry a minute ago. And again it brought thoughts of my mama, how she had loved love, too. Maybe like they said, "I get it from my mama." That tickled me. Yancey's daddy was her high school sweetheart, and Cricket's was a passionate secret affair. My daddy, she said, was on a crew building a strip mall they put up right outside of town. He was real good-natured, too; their love had been so great that they had needed but one passionate night.

"Take a look in the glove box," he said.

Steel glittered there, a gun that looked heavy, like the blowback might knock you down. My emotions swirled and fought like dust and debris in a tornado I had been sucked in. There was, above it all, the trill of fear, mostly concentrated between my legs.

"Why do you need that?"

"You never know," he said. Then, "I'm going to show you how to use it. You need to know, too."

Our first pit stop was two and a half hours down the road in Greenville because we were both yawning already. Their Xpress Mart was brightly lit and popping; a clot of loiterers looked us up and down as we passed. While I peed, he guarded the door, just in case some dude had the wrong idea, he said. We then went from aisle to aisle, picking snacks. With five dollars in my pocket and nothing else, I had not a care in the world.

"Moon Pies, Diamond? Moon Pies?" He deepened and slowed his voice. "I 'spect you need an Arra C Cola to go along with that."

I rolled my eyes. "I like Moon Pies. They're tasty."

My mama had a story she told us about how they came to

be, but I felt too shy to tell him that in the moment. I was glad when he dropped the teasing.

"Guess who else is tasty?"

"Who?" I said, batting my lashes like Betty Boop.

To answer, he grabbed me, snacks and all, and peppered my face and neck with little kisses until I squealed. A customer was looking at us, grinning for our young love.

PRISCILLA

I waited in the den for Sabre to get home from Friday evening choir rehearsal. For some reason, I was nervous like it was me who was in trouble. Honestly, I don't remember the last time Emanuel landed in any sort of formal mischief. Scuffles on the football field, maybe, but never had he failed a class or been suspended. So, all of this misbehavior was new, but considering what I had seen of him and Maggie's girl, perhaps the behavior was just new to me. At a quarter after eight, I heard Sabre's keys in the door. I heard his steps in the vestibule and called to him as he was set to pass where I sat in the den.

"Can it wait? I got a word I need you to set down."

"Absolutely not," I said. "This cannot wait."

As I spoke, he looked off in the distance and stroked the ass on his chin.

"Cilla, he said he dropped her off. Did you stop to think our son might've been telling the truth? It's not like he has a track record of this behavior. I know you have your issues with me, but not an ounce of grace for your own son is surprising."

"You had to hear his tone of voice: 'Do you think I did it?' he said, and then, 'That's not all I have to tell you.' What do you think that meant, Sabre, huh? That sure don't sound like innocence to me, and he walked right out of here when I told him not to. Lord knows I haven't been able to get his tone of voice off my mind. Or her face, Sabre. He *bit* her, dammit, he bit her hard enough to *tear her flesh*."

He appeared to be seriously mulling it over, but who knew what was going on in that vast space between his ears.

"Where is the boy now? Did Wooten leave a number? I want to call so I can get us together, and we can straighten this out as soon as possible. If it happened, it just sounds like a case of boys being boys."

"That's not at all what this is, Sabre, not at all. That poor girl looked stricken."

"Well, what are you saying, Cilla? That you believe there's something wrong with Emanuel?"

"Yes, seriously wrong, and it's been under our noses this whole time."

"Cilla, you sure you aint had one pill too many and just need to lay down?"

"No, Sabre, I'm clear as a bell, and if you don't do anything about it, there won't be anything that can be done."

"There's always something that can be done. A sermon! The Word!" he said, raising his hands like that made sense. "Find me a scripture, Cilla! Type me something good up."

6

I'm just a nobody trying to tell everybody about
somebody who can save anybody.

FROM THE MINISTER'S DESK

Sabre J. Winfrey

July 16, 2000

MORNING MESSAGE: Pay What You Weigh

SCRIPTURAL BACKGROUND: "With her enticing speech she caused him to yield, with her flattering lips she seduced him. Immediately he went after her, as an ox goes to the slaughter, or as a fool to the correction of the stocks, till an arrow struck his liver. As a bird hastens to the snare, he did not know it would cost his life." Proverbs 7:21-23 NKJV

SABRE POINTS: Who is the Bible's first seducer, and how did she change the course of human history?_____

_____

_____

How does Jesus's time in the wilderness tell us about how we can best resist temptation?_____

_____

_____

_____

List your favorite sins here._____

_____

_____

Is (see above) worth your life/afterlife?_____

_____

DIAMOND

A little after 2:00 a.m., we arrived at the Coastal Starlight Inn in Long Beach. Wonder secured us a room for fifteen dollars with an ID some white boy had made him on a recruiting trip to UT Knoxville. Our room was on the second floor at the far end; we drove down and parked. He gathered the guitar and a quilt, my bag and his, and I trudged behind him. Our room was 216, a nine, which meant good things would happen here. Inside was hot as armpits; I flipped on the light and dropped the snacks on a coffee table with its best days long behind it. The thermostat was on the other side of the door. I adjusted it, and the air chugged on dramatically. Of course, it was kind of like coming home for me. While he went into the bathroom, I plopped on the bed and found myself looking up at a mirror. The glass bore cloudy spots and a haze that made me feel I was looking at myself from some sepia-tinted era. On the nightstand was an old green phone and a coffee can covered in plaid. I reached over and tilted it toward me; inside were sticky notes, a click pen, and several gummy, red condoms.

I opened the drawer of the nightstand and found a New Testament with a photo sticking out of it. The picture featured a man in a pin-striped suit, posed like he was pushing his bowler hat onto his head. He had a broad, muscular face and what they'd call a rakish smile. I flipped the picture over: Les Daniels, taken by Shirley Daniels, "My man love his hoes, but he love me, too." I laughed out loud, and when Wonder came out of the bathroom, I showed him the picture, and he laughed, too. I put it in my wallet along with my baby doll Cornelia's birth certificate, so I could always remember this time.

After all those days without him, here he was hugging me like a pillow, and we were out here in the world like adults, and I could barely believe it, but I definitely could get used to it. For the first time in my life, I was getting exactly what I wanted. The only thing I hated was that a bad situation had driven us to this point, and that made me fear an unhappy ending. I snuggled into him, dismissed my scary thoughts, and fell asleep like a log. I woke up to a muffled morning light, freezing from breezes in and outside the room. Wonder was not in bed, but I could hear him outside.

"Who you talking to?" I said.

A voice was laughing. A female one.

"Get your ass in this room, Emanuel."

When he didn't, I leapt across that floor toward the door. He was still tilted over the railing, but by the time I stepped out on the breezeway, there was no one.

"Who were you talking to?"

"Can you smell that, Diamond? We're going to the beach."

"So you just gone ignore my question?"

"It was nothing, baby. Nobody. I promise. Can you trust me, please?"

I nodded, but I wasn't a fool, and he wasn't going to have me out here looking like one. Still, I was able to put my questions aside in the excitement of going to the beach, something I never did before. I put on the same sweats from yesterday with the T-shirt I'd slept in. The towels that came with the room weren't really beach-ready, but I rolled up the sturdiest-looking one and tucked it under my arm. Outside was like a hot wet blanket under a grim sky that seemed about to burst. He took my hand, and we dashed across four lanes of highway toward the beach. The water was like the sky but slightly darker; as we made our way closer, he stripped off his T-shirt. We found a spot and dropped the stuff.

"This a lot of water, Wonder. Is it the ocean?"

"Almost," he said.

He tugged at my sweats.

"Take these off," he said.

"And be out here in my underwear in the public?"

"Better than dragging around wet sweats."

I usually hated my skinny legs, my small chest, how they made me feel like I was still a kid, but as soon as I dropped those sweats I felt free. Like this was how people was supposed to be. I followed him in, but once I was as far as my knees, he couldn't coax me out any further.

"I got you," he said.

But I shook my head. "You remember when Dwayne tried to drag Lissandra in the pool at the picnic?"

We laughed. Lissandra fought like a cat, had everybody shocked. Dwayne ended up with a black eye.

"Well, I'm going out," he said.

He left me to swim, went so far I could see nothing but the blinding sparkle of sun on the water near where I thought he could be. I fretted until he splashed back into sight.

"DON'T DO THAT AGAIN," I screamed, punching him in his chest.

~~~~~

The first plops of rain fell as we hustled up the stairs with our grocery bags. In the breezeway, I waited impatient, chilly, as he hunted for the key. The first thing I did was to light a scented candle, red of course, to combat the musty smell that dwelled in places like these. The last thing I did after organizing the other things we'd bought was arrange my flowers in a fast-food cup, and the place went from shabby to romantically shabby. For a while, we lay completely quiet on the bed as the thunder went from grumbling to snapping, and the rain tumbled the roof. When finally it slacked, he said we were going to the pay phone to call Maggie.

"And tell her what?" I asked.

I felt so ashamed that I hadn't thought about her this whole time, knowing she must be worried sick.

"Tell her you are with me, and you are OK, and we'll be back."

I didn't want to talk to Maggie. I had always studied her face, her actions, for some kind of sign that I was a mistake, but I didn't need to see her now to know for sure I was. I'd run away from home, and all I'd been concerned about was me and Wonder and not whether she was worried or hurt or nothing. She accepted the charges and exploded.

"The coast!" she shouted. "What are you doing on the coast?"

"Mama, we just needed to get away."

"Get away? Get away from what? Neither one of you got

a damn thing to get away from. You got me to cursing again! Chanel called herself doing something like this, and I beat her from Jackson to the Dominion city limits. Let me speak to that boy."

I could hear her going off but not what she was saying. I ended the conversation promising her we would be on our way back tomorrow, but of course, we wouldn't be. Before we left for the grocery store, he went to the front office and paid for a week. For the rest of the night, we watched TV and ate pizza. It stormed all the next day. We barely left the room and spent the hours eating ice cream and making love like it was going out of style. I knew we would eventually have to go home, even though that was the last thing I wanted to do.

PRISCILLA

From the edge of sleep, I heard the phone ring, shrill, life-threatening. I smacked it one, three, four times to make it stop, but even after it went silent, the ringing in my ears continued. I squinted at the clock and saw it was almost 9:00 a.m., but I was stumped at the day of the week. The days always seemed off to me after a holiday. I came to seated, slowly, troubled by the niggling suspicion I was forgetting or had forgotten something important. I washed the sleep from my face, and feeling a little clearer, went downstairs and straight to the coffeepot.

As it percolated, an enormous yawn made me rethink getting up. I turned on the television and saw not news but cartoons. It was Saturday, and Sabre would have been at the shop almost two hours by now. The damn phone again. When I picked up the extension in the kitchen, all I heard was Maggie hollering. Loud as she was, she might as well have been standing over my shoulder. She told me her girl was gone, and the police were dealing with it like a runaway situation, and while she spoke, all the things I had disremembered resurfaced. I rolled my eyes and shook my head at my son, my husband, and most of all, myself. I placated her by telling her I was going to call Sabre and make a plan when all I wanted to do was shrug and hop right back in the bed.

The moment I hung up, a heavy, involuntary groan seeped out of me. A preliminary pain throbbed somewhere in my head. I took a deep breath, whispered a prayer, and went into his room once more. Because he was so orderly, I recognized immediately he had run away and was not just out jumping bleachers or throwing weights. His favorite guitar was absent from its stand, and so was the quilt my mama made him that would normally be folded at the end of his bed. Another groan when I found my fulfillments missing from my purse. I hunted for my stash, tore the house up like I had done for my earrings, but did not find them. Knowing the kind of day this was likely to be, I couldn't consider the implications before I'd shored myself up with some fulfillments.

Bertha answered on the first ring.

"Hey, girl," I said. "I got a mighty need. What Ty looking like?"

"Aint nobody seen hide nor hair of Ty; I been calling all week."

"He alright?"

"I'm sure he is, girl," she said, sighing. "He get in a way some-times, you know, but he never stay down. He might have checked himself in again . . . I am my brother's keeper, I guess. Leo and Mel both done passed and Glo halfway in the ground herself, and don't nobody see hifalutin Edie since she married that African."

I didn't interrupt her. I could hear the break in her voice, I knew her pain. I called Sabre at Cuts, but the phone rang unan-swered. I figured as much because Saturdays were the busiest days of the week at the shop. Even on a slow day, they were bad about picking up the phone. I bathed and called again to no answer. I hadn't been to that shop in years, but I found myself fixing my face, putting on a dress, and cracking Sabre's safe for the keys to my car. My license was still suspended, but what choice did I have? The hell if I was walking or biking up there. So when I walked in, Sherm, his number two in charge, looked at me like I had just touched down from Mars. His face drained of black and returned ashen as he stuttered out his greeting. As a matter of fact, all of them were looking at me strange.

"J-just set right there, First Lady, and Imma go get him for you."

That was when it dawned on me that something was wrong. I rushed past Sherm, Joe, Henry, and the new young barber and all the rotten niggers sitting in those chairs, rushed into my husband's office and shoved that door open to him and Katha-reen and a couple of shit-eating grins. I had no intention of hitting her. She had no idea how insignificant she was, how she was just the body of the moment. Plus, I knew she was the type that would've fastened herself to the backside of a mange-ridden wombat if she thought she could come up. She was, however, between me and my husband and caught a couple of fists in the mix. As I drove home with him trailing me, I thought about that little smirk on Kathareen's face when she saw me and how quick it got knocked off when I came in wind-milling. But that was the way the cookie crumbled when you was laying with somebody else's husband. Besides, they both deserved it, and to be honest it felt good, catching him in the act after all these years tomcatting and hound-dogging while I sat at home, raising his children. Usually, I prided myself on my ladylike qualities, but today I got gutter, and I was proud! He deserved scandal and ridicule and all the fallout.

At least they weren't fucking.

But you know they are.

I eyed him through my rearview while he trailed in his car. If looks could kill, he'd need a pine box. At home, Sabre took his time getting out. He came in while I was still peering at my stinging lip in the mirror in the foyer. I had been flailing so wildly, I'd hit myself. His eye, the one I'd popped with my ringed finger, was swollen and probably going to be bruised. Before he could sit down or tend his wounds, I told him his son had run away while he was out acting like a common gigolo.

"Cilla, I know we haven't been on the same page for a long time, but we need to get on one accord right now. Emanuel is too special a kid for us to let him let this ruin his life. Are you with me?"

I nodded.

"Can I pray with you?" he said.

We were in the huddle, the two of us; we were a team.

DIAMOND

The next morning, while Wonder was in the bathroom, there was a knock at our door. Through the peephole, I saw a skinny white chick; I swung the door open and rolled my neck.

"What do *you* want?"

She had long brown hair and wore coochie cutters with the waistband folded down. She seemed as surprised to see me as I was to see her.

"Hey, is that big boy in there?" she asked.

"The only boy in here is my man, and there is no reason you oughta be looking for him, so you best be about your merry way and don't come back."

"Aint no need for you to get smart; he's the one that asked me to come."

"Is that right? Well, you keep waiting, Becky," I said, and slammed the door in her face.

At that time, he came out of the bathroom in his swim trunks.

"What's wrong with you?" he said.

"So you friends with random white chicks now, huh?"

"Diamond, don't start nothing, won't be nothing."

"So did you invite her up here?"

"Are you going to the beach or not? If you're not ready in the next five, you're going to be sitting in this room mad by yourself."

He was leaned over tying his shoes, got up grabbing one of the beach towels we bought. Out on the breezeway he went, probably looking for that chick. I moped, but I hurried into my swimsuit and shoes. On the way over, as he walked ahead of me while not looking back, I noticed he had a complete block head. You could probably stack his head in a warehouse, I thought, and the idea of it kept me giggling. He dropped his towel and glanced back to ask me what was so funny. But I was laughing too hard, and it wasn't like I could tell him what I was thinking in the first place, which made me want to tell him anyway, and that made me laugh even more. Irritation crossed his handsome face, then calmness. He looked out toward the water with his hand shading his eyes.

"I'll take you out," he said.

Going out in the middle of that big-ass water, dangling off of his neck, was just begging to be a tally for the Reaping Season. I shook my head. He swam for a while, and we lay out for a while, and I forgot I had been mad. For lunch, we walked across the street, and I had another first: crab cakes, which I didn't really care for—too smooshy for me. Afterwards, we went right back to the beach. I had a random mystery book from the grocery store run and the little stereo from his truck. Baked brown, sun-dazed, and content, I fell into a doze. I woke up out of my nap, to see the horrible, shocking sight of the white girl strutting up the beach like she was all that. Her face and body were sunken and sickly. The long, thin, gross hair reminded me of the time I was at Pizza Hut for a birthday party and found a shock of hair someone had gotten stuck in the curlicued back of my chair. I really couldn't believe she had the nerve! She walked past me and dropped her shorts, and I watched her swim strong, sure strokes out in his direction.

How had she known I couldn't swim? She never would have the nerve to look at me like that if she thought I could follow her out and hold her under until she drowned. All I could do was watch her splash into the sun-dazzled stretch of water toward my boyfriend. I don't know how long it was before he emerged, but when he did, he was alone.

~~~~~

That evening, around eight, Wonder let the white girl in. She arrived with grocery sacks filled with snacks and liquor and a pudgy, dark boy she called her friend. Under his arms, he carried folding chairs that read: Property of Coastal Starlight. I recognized him as Mike from the front office. Although Wonder was dapping Mike up like they went way back, I didn't like the feel of this situation at all. We didn't know these damn people, and he was too smart to be trusting them. But when you had been sheltered like he had, I guess you didn't know no better. Mike was on the dresser, disabling the smoke detector. The white girl had made herself at home on the bed. It irritated me that she had already invaded his thoughts—and mine—and now she was invading our space. At least she was breaking down weed. The pale, pregnant buds looked heavenly. As she rolled, I guess she was talking to me because the boys were talking about something else.

"I turned twenty-two in March," she was saying. "I start the nursing program at GCC this fall, so I gotta get my partying out."

I took the opportunity to get a good look at her while she talked. She had pulled her hair back behind a set of gremlin ears, a mistake, and with all those lines crackling on the sides of her eyes, this chick was thirty if she was a day—nursing school, my ass.

"Uh-huh," I said.

Mike had a single gold eyetooth. He opened a big bag of off-brand nachos, which he offered around before tossing onto the bed. "You know how to play Spades, baby girl?"

"I aint your baby girl, but yes."

White girl sealed the blunt while looking at me. "Ewwww, do you always got this attitude? I thought only ugly girls had attitude like that."

Mike said, "His girl aint stupid. She know you trying to get at her stud."

I hated how everybody was laughing but me. I plucked the blunt out of Mike's hand and French-inhaled; Wonderboy looked at me, surprised. I bucked my eyes at him. I was getting pissed again thinking about this Spades game. Either the white girl would have to sit next to Wonderboy, or she got to sit across from him as his partner and be in his face all night.

"First, you gone play that guitar for us, Mr. Wonderboy?" she asked.

I hated how she was too comfortable with him, and the fact that he seemed to be eating it up irked my soul even more. He was telling her about the guitar being a gift to his father, and it was something very *Roots*-y about the whole thing. And then: the way he hopped his ass up and grabbed that guitar with no hesitation. Whereas I had to twist his arm for him to sing, Trailerina asked him one time, and he jumped ready to strum his thumbs loose and trill like a canary. You know what?

Despite the fact that I'd seen him sing in church for years, I didn't connect that with performance. But then I realized that he *was* a performer, was born and bred to be, and that meant the performer and the person doing the performing were not the same. He had his eyes toward me, but I knew the show was all for the white girl. He sang: *If I had a wish, baby, I'd wish that he never left you feeling like this* . . . He knew it was one of my favorite songs, and as always, his singing broke me down. I was right along with them, swaying at the delight of his melodious depths, the way his magic fingers coaxed the music from the strings.

When he was done, Mike said, "Man, if I had your hand, I'd throw mine in right now."

No, you wouldn't, I thought, and smirked. Wonder was looking at me, had caught my expression. I wanted to know what he was thinking, but this was not the time to ask. The girl broke me out of my thoughts.

"Sing something else."

"No," he said, more firmly than I would have expected, and I recognized his team-leader voice.

He placed the guitar in its case and leaned the case against the nightstand.

"Cheers to you, Mr. Wonderboy. You have to have a drink after that," she said.

"He doesn't drink," I told them.

"Aw, mama, let this mane be great!" Mike said this, as he was already pouring vodka and pink lemonade in red cups.

Wonder took the cup and began sipping. When the blunt came around, he acted like he was going to try that, too.

"You don't know what you're doing," I cautioned him.

As if to prove my point, he inhaled too deep and was thrown into a long series of barking coughs. I whacked him on the back. This time everybody was laughing but him. His eyes were bloodshot over the rim of his cup.

"Mr. Wonderboy, your new name is Virgin Mary," said the white girl.

Mike got the notepad from the Folgers can and drew the scoring grid. It was Wonder's turn at the blunt again. He imitated the way I did it, and this time he got it right. I had to hand it to white girl, though; her card skills were on point. We watched, mesmerized, as she shuffled and whizzed out cards like a professional.

"Aint been no nigger beatings around these parts in a while. I guess I get to do some tonight."

Again, everyone else laughed, but I didn't.

PRISCILLA

Diamond had called from a pay phone down on the coast. While Sabre tried to get someone who could figure out exactly where they were, I made myself a quick drink, which unfortunately turned out to be the last of the bottle. I took a good, long swallow, but the second, I swished around in my mouth. Tiptoeing without knowing exactly why, perhaps because of the heft of the quiet, I went into Manny's bedroom. For some reason, I got caught up in his pictures: with the governor at some state football scholar-athlete banquet . . . with the mayor for student of the month. One of his sophomore year, volunteering with the Special Olympics, where he held two special kids' hands up and shouted, "We're all champions," right before the photo was snapped by the *Clarion Ledger*. Grinning like a Cheshire cat on a picture with B. B. King (the boys had opened for him in the '93 and '94 Delta Jubilees). Sabre had always claimed their guitar skills came from his side, but everybody knew my side was kin to the Hemphills, so we had skills, too. I said all that to sigh this: Manny was one special boy, but I had long known his cabbage was done, while his cornbread was soft in the middle.

Slowly, I spun around, taking in what might have been the neatest teen boy's room in all the history of civilization, simultaneously scouring it and my mind for information, for clues. He'd had a birthday cake every year, a party on each highlight year. (Four birthday parties a year were out of the question.) There was homecooked food whenever he wanted it, lavish Christmases, kisses and snuggles until he outgrew them. I had been in the bleachers at every game since he had been playing youth league football, been anywhere he'd ever sung or played a note. Yes, I drank a little and took a fulfillment once in a while, but I had showed up! And for that matter, Sabre had, too. How had we spoiled him?! When there was so much he did right!

I *had* shaken him once—on a day when the bread was burning in the broiler, and he was teething, and Ivy had made a drum of something in the living room. Manny had screamed and flailed so that he almost flung himself out of my arms, and I shook him to get him to understand not to do that. It wasn't enough to hurt him, just enough to shock him, and I did hug him and apologize, dammit! Maybe that caused his soft spot to rot. Shit, I don't know. I don't remember shaking any of my other boys, but, hell, I had forgotten (or blocked) so much in my life that I could be lying to myself.

I was on board with Sabre. I guess I had to be, right? What kind of woman would I be if I willingly let this ruin his potential? Would I turn him in to a lynch mob, banging at the door to hang him if he had winked at a white woman? Because if I made him face his day in court on the lines of accountability and whatnot, that's precisely what I'd be doing. And for what? Folk born to be victims? I would never hear the end of it from the community or my sons or my family, and this would disrupt our entire lifestyle. I could see Melvistine wagging her jowly face as she spread the news. I saw us losing everything and people like the Wootens looking down on us as we got it out of the mud. I couldn't place myself there, couldn't sit with myself in it. I sighed, topped off my drink. Was the kind of woman who made her boy accountable better and braver than me? Naw, honestly right now, despite what I thought of the son or the father, I needed ease and to do what was best for me, and it would definitely be easier to sweep his transgressions under the rug than allow ours to be brought to light.

DIAMOND

I woke chilly and alone on the bed. The quiet was too quiet. I pushed up onto one elbow, looked around the room, and frowned; it was trashed. Someone had puked, which I didn't remember at all. The bathroom door was ajar, but the room was unlit. I went there, expecting to see him slumped over the tub or toilet, wasted, but he was not. I ran to the door, yanked it open, and saw his truck was missing. Rushed, frantic and barefoot, down the breezeway, trying to locate it, but neither the truck nor Wonder was to be found. Before I knew it, I was bawling, heading back toward 216, not knowing what else to do. At first, I was upset at myself for being weak and silly, but I soon realized these weren't regular tears; these were fire and poison. The chill that hovered in the room made his absence even deeper. While I fiddled with the ancient thermostat, I spotted a half-empty bottle of vodka on the coffee table and drank some. I was sick with the realization of how vulnerable love had made me once again. I had followed him here with no money of my own, no transportation, not knowing anybody but him, and that had made no sense at all on my part. And yet and still, I didn't want to call Maggie and admit it. I lay down and wrapped my arms around myself.

I woke the second time, hot and blinking at the brightness of the room. I was shocked by the time: 3:09, and the fact that I was still alone. Where the hell was he? Had him and that girl got married? Had her and Mike robbed and murdered him? That would mean he was another tally for the Reaping Season, and I would be left to explain to all of Dominion. I decided to walk down to the beach and check for him there. I put on my shoes to head out, and when I opened the door, he was sitting beside it, legs outstretched, head down on his chest. I stooped to examine him. There was a lump on the top of his head; his breathing was ragged but loud. I shook him, called his name, but he didn't respond. I slapped him with as much strength as I could muster; his eyes popped open, questioning. He gingerly touched his head, winced.

"You OK? Can you get up?"

He nodded. I hoisted and he heaved, and we got him inside and onto the couch. He scanned the scrambled room.

"Where is Sarah?"

I shrugged.

Wild-eyed and crunk, he lurched to his feet so fast it scared me. I had seen him do this more than once after being knocked flat on the football field by some country bloke out of Starkville or Panola. He snatched open the door, and that was when he noticed his missing truck. The howl that came out of him was loud, stark, and striking. I took him by the waist and led him to the bed; he fell backwards, covered his face with his hands.

"Oh, Lord, Diamond, what am I going to tell my daddy?"

I felt a little sorry for him when he started crying, but to be honest, that spoiled boy thing was getting to me. I knew hunger so deep that it was like a friend; it took me two years to stop hoarding food when I moved into Maggie's. His truck was gone, but it was insured. The two or three hundred that was in his wallet was nothing to him. Even if his childhood did have some problems, his whole life had been filled with people going out of their way to make him comfortable. He was right to be sick about the guitar, but, hey, he was the one doing the most trying to impress that foot-faced girl. He had the nerve to be all sad-sack, without once considering how his foolishness put me at risk. Even after all that, his parents would forgive him. Even after all that, I had already forgiven him.

I sat patiently, holding him until he stopped crying. He

asked me to step out, so he could call home. I went down to the beach and waded in the water. Nearby, tangled up in the weedy grass was a plastic grocery sack and the plastic ring from a six-pack of something. Dominion High's chemistry teacher, Mr. Croft, was on loan from Oregon. He told us to snip these rings before throwing them into the trash because animals could find them and make nooses out of them. In class, I didn't know why he put it that way. Some kids thought he said it like that to be racist because we were in Mississippi, but it made me think of some depressed duck, swimming solemnly over to the rings somebody irresponsibly left, ready to end it all. The gun in the glove box crossed my mind, and the next thing I knew, I was kicking rocks trying to get to Wonder.

Three panting blocks to the motel, one flight of stairs—I launched myself up the last two, flew at the door of our room. My hands fumbled the key in the lock, but I got the door open. He looked like he was sleeping at first, but there was something foamy coming from his lips. I pounced, felt his wrist, found a feeble pulse. My knee caught what I immediately knew to be a pill bottle. I reached for it: Midas T. Benny, it read. Take as needed. Dr. H. Booker. I was proud of how calm my words came out to the dispatch.

"I'm in room 216 at the Coastal Starlight; my boyfriend is unconscious. I think he took some pills. Please get here now."

~~~~~

A paramedic was shoving something up his nose, and at first, I thought they would kill him trying to save him.

"Don't hurt his voice," I said, with the thinnest of cracks in mine.

I was trying to monitor them, but some officer was asking me questions at the same time. Plus, shivers kept running my body, and I was dizzy. I did catch the brawny-armed responders transferring Wonder from the bed to the stretcher with textbook form. I knew this because when we lived in the Sunflower, we never missed an episode of *Rescue 911*. When he was gone, and the room had cleared, it all fell on me, and so I called Maggie collect. As I explained to her what had happened, I spotted the notepad; printed on it in his neat writing were the following words: My apology. I tried to hear it come naturally in his voice but failed. Tracing the letters kept me from crying as I spoke to Maggie. She didn't curse or yell at me; however, the flatness in her voice might have been worse. When we hung up, I went through his duffel bag. There were two loose twenties and a book with the Joker's name in it. I hid the book in my purse, and with the twenties, I called a cab for the hospital, disobeying Maggie's orders to stay put. Right before I left the room for the last time, I looked at the little home we had made, destroyed by those creeps in just one night. Then, for some reason, I opened the drawer and put Les Daniels's picture back in the New Testament.

PRISCILLA

I was ready to go, but Rev was shirtless and going back and forth from his study to his bedroom, dropping items on the bed as he passed, as if we were going on vacation instead of the hospital. Emanuel could be drawing his last breaths at this very moment, and here his daddy was messing around.

"What is all this for, Sabre? We don't have time for this. We have a six-hour drive!"

"The boy is stable," he said, "and the good Lord already told me, this sickness is not unto death."

He had assembled various bottles and brushes, a leather bag with clippers, a dopp kit, a garment bag. His cologne stood in the places he was not. I followed him into his closet, where he pulled on a crisp shirt and inserted a clerical collar.

"Should I get your smock, too? You gone do the doctor's hair when we up there, Sabre?"

"Be serious, woman. Things have happened in my home; things have come into my home while my back was turned, and Luke 9:1 give me the power and the authority to cast them out. In the name of Jesus, I will cast them out. I must have the proper tools for that."

"And the fourth verse," I said, "says take nothing for the journey."

He ignored me to get on his knees in front of the bed. His shoulders seemed as strong, if not stronger, than they were the time I sat up on them in 1970, years before those boys started coming. Of course, he was thinner then; everybody was skinny in the seventies. That was so forever ago; a tune snuck into my mind, a bit about time slipping, slipping into the future. He used this song sometimes in the benediction to let folk know how imminent the need for salvation was.

"Father God," he said, "please, grant us traveling grace on

the highways and byways. Still my wife's tongue and steady my mood. Hold my son in your bosom till I can put my hands on him, and when I get there, I ask you to shift his atmosphere. Break every yoke that is not of you. Heal, deliver, and set free. We count it done by faith in your son Jesus's name. Amen."

When we were finally on the highway, I filled him in on the entire situation with his son. I was unsatisfied with his calmness and the repeated *Is that so*'s and *unh-hunh*s. Soon, the car went silent, and the anger and worry that burned inside of me did not fade.

"You know this is your doing here," I said. "You're always pressuring him to this or that. You never just let him be."

"To whom much is given, much is due. And, besides, it wasn't me asking him to sing at every other sorority meeting and such."

"Who let him watch his dog die?"

"Where you think he got the pills from?"

7

I'm just a nobody trying to tell everybody about
somebody who can save anybody.

FROM THE MINISTER'S DESK
Sabre J. Winfrey

July 23, 2000

MORNING MESSAGE: The Mighty Will Be Brought Low

SCRIPTURAL BACKGROUND: "Hell from beneath is excited about
you, to meet you at your coming; it stirs up the dead for
you, all the chief ones of the earth; it has raised up
from their thrones all the kings of the nations. They all
shall speak and say to you: 'Have you also become as weak
as we? Have you become like us? Your pomp is brought down
to Sheol, and the sound of your stringed instruments; the
maggot is spread under you and worms cover you.'" Isaiah
14:9-11 NKJV

SABRE POINTS: How is death the great equalizer?_____
_____

In the story of the rich man and Lazarus, the rich man asks
Abraham to allow Lazarus to dip his finger in cool water
to parch the rich man's tongue. Why can he not?_____
_____

What do these passages tell us of the nature of hell?____
_____

False religions speak of a halfway point between heaven
and hell. How does the Christian know that to be untrue?
_____
_____

DIAMOND

Something had happened in the emergency room. From some form of consciousness, he had struggled and fought with the paramedics. He was strong as a bull, one of the nurses said. He had to be brought to life and then sedated. I was exhausted from waiting. Then finally they let me see him and I was jittery on my way to the room. I eased the heavy door open, as if not to scare him. His face was swollen and soft; his body, outlined by the thin, white blanket, was still but held the shape of a pounce. I covered his chest with mine, felt the ambitious thud of his heart. Suddenly, he raised his shoulders off the bed and went down again. He was moving his mouth, but only a thin, whistly, spitty sound came out.

"Wonder, are you trying to say something? What, baby? What? Talk to me."

But he had settled down. I wanted to lie in bed with him and soothe him. But he was hooked to stuff, and there was always a nurse or aide passing by. I settled for scooting the chair as close as it would go to the bed, laying my head near his hip, and stretching my arm along the side of his body. As uncomfortable as the position was, I stayed just that way. I needed him to know he was not alone. I had to move when the nurse came in and checked something, but immediately after she left, I returned to his side.

I didn't know what I would do if he died. Sure, I should expect the worst, considering what had happened in my life so far, but I just couldn't. He had to make it. There had to be something in this world that would be mine for good. I remembered last fall when he took me to the Delta Jubilee downtown. The streets were packed with locals and people from the tristate area. We were having fun until he asked me:

"Why do you do that?"

"Do what?"

"Be all up in people faces like that, especially men—what are you looking for?"

I stuttered, embarrassed, but eventually gave him a random excuse. I didn't know why, but I couldn't explain to him I did it because any of those people could be somebody I loved and hadn't seen in years. That I hadn't lost hope that my mother might be walking around here, maybe with amnesia or something. But I felt too silly and embarrassed and flawed to say that. Anyway, how do you explain this to someone like him, who'd never slept in a car at the park or missed one single meal, whose family tree hadn't been hacked at every branch? I wanted to shake him awake and tell him I'd never again be staring in other folks' faces for family; my family would be him.

~~~~~

Someone was calling my name, nudging me gently. I raised my head from the pillow I'd made of my arms and peered up at the First Lady. It took me a moment to recognize her. She wore baggy clothes that I never would have imagined her in, and there were large, dark circles under her eyes. The Reverend, in slacks and a crisp button-down, was at Wonder's other side, holding his hand.

"Thank you," she said. "Thank you."

She hugged me, but I felt stiff and surprised at their presence, as if I wasn't the one who had sounded the alarm. Their arrival meant that this time was truly over, and as sour as it had ended, the magical quality of the bit of stolen adulthood remained. It was the end of my hope that all this could somehow be undone, and we could somehow reclaim the joy and excitement we felt on our way here or in the love we'd made. That would never be again.

"What made him do this, Diamond?" asked the First Lady. "The doctor said he had contusions on his head. The police said he was robbed. What happened?"

"I wasn't in the room when he took the pills," I said. "But other stuff happened before that, stuff he didn't tell me about."

Their gazes were focused, waiting for me to elaborate. Facts rumbled around, threatening to loosen my tongue, but I shook my head. It might seem silly, but I didn't want them to think bad of him. The First Lady sighed and refocused on her son. Without looking at me, she said, "We are going to get you to the bus station tomorrow. Maggie is worried sick."

"I want to stay with him," I told them. "I have to."

"They're going to want to give him some kind of evaluations," said the Reverend. "It might take days."

"I want to be with you when you take him back."

"I'll check with Maggie, but I can't make no promises," the First Lady said. "I must ask that you not betray him when we get home."

I was stunned that she could say or think such a thing, and I wanted to snap back, but staring into her eyes was like staring into Wonder's, so instead, I put my hand up like I was taking an oath. "I know you think we are young, but I told him I would love him forever no matter what, and I meant it." She nodded like she agreed with me, but her expression didn't match, like she knew something I didn't.

PRISCILLA

After speaking to the doctor, Rev left the bedside vigil to call the other boys. When he didn't return right away, I knew he was pacing the halls or walking up and down the stairs; he'd never been able to sit still for any length of time. In half an hour, he was back. I told him to get the girl a hotel, but she shook her head.

"I'm sorry to say this," she said, "but yall will not be who he wants to see when he first wakes up."

And I knew what she said was true.

"Do you need something?" I asked her.

"Um . . . some food?"

"Child, you haven't been out of this hospital all day, have you? Oh, Lord, not on my watch. Maggie would have my hide. Rev, take Diamond. I want to sit with him a while. I doubt he'll wake up before yall get back."

"Oh, no, ma'am," the girl said, "I'll just take some chips or something."

"Don't no-ma'am me—no telling what kind of dirt you and him here have been eating these past couple of days. I am going to make sure you get some good meals in you, starting now."

"It's almost midnight," Sabre said. "What's open?"

"There's a place not far from the beach," she said, and picked up her purse.

On her way out, she touched Manny's hand, and as she passed me, I caught her in a hug, but her arms stayed at her sides. She was thin, but not frail, much sturdier than I expected; in the embrace, her chin landed on top of my head.

"Thank you," I said.

She nodded. I watched them leave and then lay like she had been, arms stretched across his body. I knew one thing: I needed fulfillments in my system, and I couldn't help but think that I was in a place full of them, none of which I could get my hands on. It was like being thirsty with nothing around but sea-water. Manny's rest was fitful, and his mouth was moving but no words. I wanted to talk this time. I wanted to understand him.

"Tell me, baby. Tell Mama."

I willed him to wake up, to look me in the eye, to honor me with that, after all the mess he'd caused, the stinking mess to be waded through and corrected and swept away, but he refused.

DIAMOND

The Reverend opened doors for me, like Wonder would have. While buckling my seat belt, I realized I had only seen him from a distance—either in the clerical robes that made him seem like a fortress or slick and starched in a suit with his hand stuck out for somebody to shake. Even on the sidelines of the football games, in a baseball cap, he read as fresh and coolheaded. At that moment and up close, he seemed smaller, less certain. The drive was silent until his voice rumbled out of the dark, surprising me.

"Daughter, relieve your burden. Speak if you know something."

For a minute, I wondered if he meant daughter, as in daughter in Christ or daughter-in-law? Either way, I knew my loyalty.

"You're not helping him by keeping things from us. It will only prevent him from getting the help he needs."

I shrugged, turned toward the window. He found the waffle place without my help; everything was on the same major street, just like at home. The interior of the restaurant was so cold the windows dripped with sweat. I wrapped my arms around myself because I knew if I started to tremble, tears were close behind, and I wasn't about to be crying in front of this man.

"You cold?"

I said no, lying, but he offered me his big, boxy jacket anyway, and I hung it across my shoulders. It smelled great, of leather and sweet with something ancient in the background, as if the Reverend knew actual frankincense dealers from the outskirts of Bethlehem.

"Get whatever you want."

He pulled out a little pad and was making notes on something. Even though he was old, the young waitress didn't take her eyes off him when I was ordering. I kept peeking, too. Everybody always said Wonder looked just like the First Lady, but I saw the resemblance was only superficial: his face, the bones and composition of it were from his daddy. And although the Reverend didn't have gray eyes, his had the same quality of being able to see through to the bone of you. The face wasn't so much handsome as it was strong, like if the world fell into ruin after World War III, the tribes would still choose him to lead.

PRISCILLA

The three of us spent a chilly, sporadic night in Manny's room. I woke first, rubbing a crick out of my neck, thinking surely there was no night longer than one spent in a hospital. The girl dozed in the chair by Manny's bed, and Sabre snored softly from the small pullout we shared. I was rousing him as the nurse came in. Later, when the girl was out talking to Maggie, I asked him if he recalled how we met. I had never been big on reflection—since the activity had always only served to alert me when and to what extent I'd been a fool, but I sat in front of him, caressing that old mushy stuff in my mind. Considering all we had in the mix at the moment, I felt silly for feeling so sentimental for that time and the strength of that love, whether perceived or actual.

You remember, I was standing in the lot of Annie Ruth's Grill with three plates of barbecue, waiting for my brother to come for me. My hair was long and hot on the back of my neck. I had on that halter dress with loud orange stripes and kept sipping out of my brother's iced tea to refresh myself. I will always remember how that tea was icy and amputation sweet, and that when I gave it to my brother, it was half gone. I

DOMINION

was 'bout to take a seat on the bench up front when you came
up behind me.

"I just bought my sister a doll baby for her birthday that
wasn't half so pretty as you," you said.

"Was that the best you could do?" I asked, looking you up
and down and smiling inside because I didn't want to let on that
I saw something I liked.

You grinned, though. "That was the best I could say, but
the best I could do would be to give you everything your heart
desire."

"That was much better," I said.

"I've been watching you waiting out here. Is there somewhere you want me to run you? That's my automobile over
there."

You pointed to a big, cream something. I wasn't a girl who
paid much attention to things like that back then, but I became
that and worse. I couldn't help but notice how nice you were
dressed and how you smelled. You had a part cut in the middle
of your head, and you smiled, showing those gapped teeth you
gave all the boys. Your trademark, you called it.

"How old are you?" I asked.

"Twenty-four, and you, doll?"

"Twenty-one on my birthday," I said.

"Was or will be? What's your name? And you didn't answer
my other question. Can I see you home?"

"You sure have a lot of questions, sir."

"Well, if you act right, one can be *Will you marry me?*"

I started laughing again, flipped my hand to dismiss you like
you were talking nonsense. You caught my hand and kissed it.

When you did that, I noticed how big your fingers were, how useful they looked. When I saw my brother easing on up the block, my confidence began to leak. You stood in front of me, looking righteous, and I was scared of what you would think when you saw my bad hip.

"Well, sir, that's my ride coming up now."

"At least let me carry your bag," you said.

The car was only a few steps away, and I willed you not to notice my lopsided walk, but you did.

"Oh, you're even more special than I thought, doll baby— you got an angel on your hip."

"You remember telling me that?"

His eyes had glazed over. I felt pitiful because I was begging him to remember that he'd once loved and seen me, while realizing that he had perhaps never done either of those things. That maybe he'd only needed a vessel for his legacy and deemed me appropriate, and it was not enough to keep him interested in me. The sad part was that it had never in the history of the world been enough; the saddest part was that so many women like me had convinced themselves it was noble to participate. I shook my head.

"I can't believe I thought you took them vows as seriously as I did. You courted me knowing good and well you didn't want a wife, you wanted a worshipper. My bad, you wanted *worshippers*. Tuh! And all those kinds of women you claimed to disdain, you sho have flowers for. Now, look at the mess that we made because you lied from the beginning."

"Cilla, I'm going to fix all of this."

He was talking with his hands. He had useful hands, thick

fingers to build and tease and squeeze. When we met, I knew these hands could make me a home, except I didn't know they would rip it up as well.

"Oh, there's nothing to fix for us, but our boy, he's got something wrong with him, and it's deep wrong. Sabre, why would that girl lie on him? Why would he have a missing man's property?"

"Boys gone be boys, Cilla, so don't blow things out of proportion. It's a righteous explanation for all of this. We can work on it, Cilla, I promise."

DIAMOND

Wonder came to, wanting water. His voice sounded raspy, but maybe that was because he said his throat hurt. Rev. Winfrey ran for the doctor. When the medical crew arrived, the First Lady stayed, but they shooed us into the hallway. The Reverend was crying.

"I just can't understand how it came to this, but Imma fix it. Jesus, with your help, Imma fix it."

I rolled my eyes at his ignorance. He didn't know because he was just looking and not seeing. If he couldn't get that, I didn't know what to tell him. People rarely just snap and do crazy shit. What looked like a snap to other people was actually an erosion of the surfaces that we built up for protection, and unfortunately people would rather dwell on the snap than the wearing. I had learned from my mama, and in that, I understood that anybody was capable of almost anything on any day, and for that I couldn't judge Wonder. I realized what the First Lady was trying to say with that look she gave me when I said I would love him forever. She was thinking that we wouldn't last because we were young, or that I didn't know any better, but I *did* know our love would never be old and busted like theirs. And I *did* know I would carry his secrets to the grave, and I wouldn't be trapped in the past like Lot's wife. After the doctors cleared out, the Reverend and I rushed in. Wonder's eyes fixed on me at once.

"Diamond," he said.

The tone told me everything I needed to know. I rushed to his side, wanting to choke, kiss, and fuss all at the same time. But we just stared at each other like the others weren't even in the room.

PRISCILLA

Dr. Nichols said Emanuel could remember everything or nothing from the past couple of weeks. He could remember it all weeks or years from now or in a dream. That's because there had been MDMA and the painkillers in his system, letting me know he had to have been slipped something. All in all, the doctor said he was a strong boy and very lucky. When they rolled him back in the room from the tests they did on him, he already looked better. Soon, he fell asleep again. I sat by his bedside, watched his peaceful face. Before he'd flinched and fought, but now he rested as peacefully as a baby. I glanced at Sabre.

"Will they commit him?"

"I'm not sure," he said.

"What yall mean?" the girl asked.

We both turned toward her. I had forgotten she was in the room. "If you attempt suicide, you often have to be evaluated to make sure you're not a danger to yourself or others. Sometimes they have to take you to a special hospital; since he's a minor, they might hold him here. It just depends on what the doctor says."

"Do you think he is a danger?" she said. When I didn't answer, she went: "You don't know him then. He would only hurt someone if he had to. He's one of the sweetest boys at school."

The Wooten girl popped in my mind. I remembered those teeth marks on her cheek, the jaunty way that boy came downstairs and smiled at her with those same teeth. Did I tell Diamond that? The same one I asked not to betray him? He had lorded over this little clown while pissing seed on her belly, and she still wouldn't understand if I, his mama, insisted her best bet was to stay as far away from this beautiful monster as she possibly could. Could a mother say that? Should I? The right answer failed me at that moment, but I did know it was time out for this foolishness.

"You're gonna be on the first thing smoking to Dominion tomorrow."

"She's pregnant," Manny said. "A girl named Sonja."

"Oh, God," I groaned.

Diamond gasped. "That's my mother's name. I never told him that. I haven't even said her name out loud in years . . ."

Lord, I had a mighty need. I wished I could call Bertha, just in case Tyrone *had* shown up, but at the very least, Sabre was going to have to get me some liquor up in here. This situation, in its entirety, had shaken me, and as well, it had shaken away all my need for pretense.

"I was in hell, Daddy," he said.

"The doctor said you might be confused, son," Sabre said in a soft, thoughtful tone, one he probably only used with Kathareen. He put his hand on the boy's shoulder. "Do you remember what happened? Tell us what you remember."

"Did that white girl do something to you?" Diamond blurted.

"What white girl?" Sabre and I went at the same time.

"What white girl?" said Manny.

"One of yall need to get to explaining quick."

But he got very drowsy after that. Sabre started to adjust his pillow, just as his eyes were drifting closed. I was going to get to the bottom of this if I had to shake it out of this girl.

"Start talking, Diamond," I said.

"But, First Lady," she said in a voice that was soft, yet cheeky, "didn't you say not to betray him?"

I'd've had her helicoptered out of here right then if I didn't know the chaos lurking behind her sweet expression. Come hell or high water, though, I was going to put a stop to whatever this thing was they had going on. In the meantime, I would pray to high heaven that this girl was not actually pregnant. She was all big eyes and excitement.

"Does this mean we get to have a wedding before the baby comes?"

DIAMOND

With the Winfreys and I being on the coast, we all missed church on the Second Sunday. They were absent the next Sunday, too. Maggie had dragged me there against my will, even though these nosy folk been wagging their heads and tongues on us for almost two weeks. All of it was just speculation because no one knew the truth but me, and I hadn't said anything to anybody. The whole service, I felt heat on the back of my neck, and I wished I had put on one of Maggie's hats or at least not put my hair in this tight bun. Without even one of the First Family in the building, the place was strange, like the roof had gotten higher but the walls had closed in. Rev. Neely brought the message, but he lacked Rev. Winfrey's charisma, and he couldn't sing.

All the next week, I waited for my period to come, but it did not. I thought about Wonder's prophesy and was filled with a peace, a reassurance that I needed to combat the fear of my dreams coming true.

That Saturday, Maggie bought me a test, and we didn't have to wait the three minutes because the second line came up at the same time as the first. I shrugged. I couldn't tell what Maggie felt by her expression. I didn't know what to say.

"I guess you could've chosen worse," she said, sighing.

Later, from my bed, I could hear her speaking with the Winfreys, so I crept up to her bedroom door to eavesdrop. When I heard they were planning a meeting, my heart skipped a beat. I had not seen him since we got back—they had kept us apart—so it comforted me that even though it wouldn't be like it was, I still had him in me. And soon, so soon, I would get to lay eyes on him. A lot could happen in a couple of days, and I needed to know if he still loved me.

〜〜〜

On Fourth Sunday, we were late, walked in in the middle of the devotional being rendered by a familiar voice.

"I want to know who is, who is worthy . . ."

The quartet picked up the chorus as we found seats at the back. I saw right away Emanuel was missing and that the First Lady was not in her regular spot behind the mourning bench, though Ivy and Mack rounded out the musicians. The Reverend was still not himself, I could tell; his voice sounded sad and hollower to me, if that made any sense. Was it silly that I wanted him to acknowledge me in some way? I mean, I had saved his son's life and had not uttered a word of their secrets to anybody. But, of course, he didn't. When it was time for the sermon, I felt the electric anticipation of the congregation running through me, too. Instead of singing the hymn, he talked, prompting Mr. Watson to lower the volume of the organ.

"I pride myself on being a man who addresses, rather than avoids, so here I am, bowed in front of you for the purpose of confession."

His voice had come out rumbly; he cleared his throat.

"To my brothers and sisters in Christ, I come to bring you a word that's not of God's heart but of my own. I could've gotten up here and given you excuses and explanations, but I'm not. What I am giving you is an apology. For overstepping the boundaries of my power. For indulging the desires of my flesh. For missing the problems in my own life, while proselytizing to you. What I am saying to you is that effective immediately, I will be stepping down from the leadership of the Seals to work on my personal house in obedience to God and family. A blind shepherd will lead his flock off a cliff, but a man of God won't stay willfully blind—he will seek the light, and that's what I'm doing. Now, I don't want yall to wait on me, neither. My mistakes aint no cause for you all to suffer. Pastor Sayles, Rev. Espy, Rev. Neely—any of them could stand in my stead, and you wouldn't miss a thing, and you might get something new. So, I'm moving aside, but I will still be an active member, and if yall still want me to preach sometimes, I will. Know I love all of you, and I love the Seals."

The congregation erupted. Rev. Winfrey raised his hands and quieted the people.

"The decision is made. Yall, stay for the Word."

With that, he stepped out of the pulpit and out of the side door. Rev. Espy stood with his hands up to a chorus of boos. Mrs. Kathareen, who looked exquisite in a vibrant floral dress, was crying like her heart was breaking. Ms. Bertha was a loud whisperer; she nudged Maggie, saying Kathareen should have stayed at home, like I wished I could have, seeing that people were talking about me, too.

"Kat's an awful dangerous woman." Ms. Bertha chuckled.

"'Cause you know a man gone man," said Maggie.

I had never thought of women as dangerous before. But the white girl was definitely dangerous—she had circled Wonder like a shark and left him bleeding in the water. And then there was Mrs. Kathareen, whose kick pleats and pointy heels had brought down the church. Dangerous women had the power to make men risk it all; they brought men to their knees. What was the source of that power? Did I have it? Did I want it? *Should I want it?* I slumped even lower in the pew. I was tired of thinking, was tired period. Worst of all, school was starting in just over a week, and I was going to have to deal with being pregnant in high school and everything that went with it. I couldn't wait to go home and lay down.

8

PRISCILLA

Bertha called the day before Halloween to say they had discovered what was left of Tyrone's body in the woods of Coahoma County. Ivy had moved back in after we brought Manny from the coast; I had him take me to sit with her the next day, like she did when my people passed. I carried her a lemon picnic pound cake and a bank envelope that I set on the coffee table, where there was a pile of such offerings. Dust and shadows had gathered in her home, were revealed when I opened the blinds. I settled beside her on the couch and took her hands into mine.

"How you feeling, Bert?"

She said, "Like a bear, making tracks and going nowhere."

"I'm so so sorry."

"You didn't do it."

A moment of silence passed; she smacked her hands down onto her thighs, remembering something.

"How you feeling about that grandbaby? It's the best part of motherhood to me." She managed a laugh.

"It's earlier than I thought but not as early as it could have been," I said, "considering I had all them boys with they daddy blood. But I'm getting excited."

A small lie. I really wanted to tell her (or anybody for that matter) that between this batty girl and my brutal boy, I had a sneaking suspicion they were birthing the Antichrist. But you just couldn't lay that kind of thing on people.

"You're going to adore that baby."

"Uh-huh," I said. To change the subject, I glanced down Bertha's quiet, dark hall. "Quincy back there asleep?"

"At work. Girl, him and Ty didn't much get along in the first place. You know I aint naïve—I can see how somebody might want to kill him—maybe he owed money or broke into their house—I don't know. I just can't see how they could kill him and dump him to be picked over by animals like that. At least let his people have something to bury. You know we was always scared they would send him back in pieces from over there in Iraq, but not here at home, naw, not here at home."

I sat and listened to her talk about her baby brother, how he didn't start off awry and how smart he was in school. He wrote for the school newspaper, she said, loved to write. At that, I thought of the notebook in Manny's possession, and my heart turned a little somersault. Neither Sabre nor I had pressed him for information since the hospital, because the doctor suggested we give him time to recover memories on his own instead of running the risk of inserting false ones. And what would information do anyway, other than make it all real? As long as he had no memory, I had no real knowledge, and as long as I had no real knowledge, I wasn't a hypocrite for my behavior, or even worse, responsible. What was I supposed to do anyway? Go up to the police station or up to Artie and say, "My son might have killed Tyrone Benny"? With no evidence whatsoever? What about my other sons? What would they think of me if I did that?

"Please ask Rev to say a few words over Ty. All we doing is graveside. You know Espy been funking it up every Sunday, with his stuttering ass. I hope they don't throw him out on his head before Rev can get back in the pulpit."

"I'll see what I can do tonight, girl."

"I got a couple of nerve pills," she said out of the blue. "I know you need them."

"You need them yourself," I said.

I took them anyway. Then I was saved by the bell—another visitor. I called Ivy, and I hugged my friend and left. At home, Ivy went straight into the den, where his brother and father were slapping their knees and tee-heeing about something. In this great, big old mess, how could they find something so amusing? The bones of a person they knew had been recovered, my dearest friend's brother. Manny could be a laughing murderer—did that not strike fear in Sabre?

"What's so funny?"

For a moment, I stared open-mouthed at them, and they stared back like blank-faced triplets.

"Ma, chill," one of the lot said.

"*Ma, chill?*" I parroted.

"Yes, chill, Cilla," said Sabre, with a smug, slappable expression on his face.

At that, I turned on my heel and headed upstairs. The fulfillments from Bertha crossed my mind, and I felt better and worse at the same time. I went into my closet for reinforcements, then remembered Bertha asked me to ask Sabre about speaking at Ty's fune and groaned. I dreaded asking him for anything; I didn't want to talk to him at all, but speaking over

Ty was the least he could do, considering Ty was technically a member, and Sabre was technically still the pastor. Above my head were stacks of shoes in clear plastic boxes, and surrounding me were suits and pants and dresses, some cloaked beneath dry cleaner's plastic, some with tags still attached. How had I accumulated so much? When? Why? I realized these things, including my mindset, were the required accoutrements of a First Lady. I was ready to leave that costume on the floor of my life. I wouldn't type another program or order another magnolia spray for the foyer. I would relinquish my corner of the second pew. I hoped the next woman filled it better.

I swept a row of floral-patterned hatboxes down. I was done with these helmets of salvation. Not only did I not want to be First Lady, I didn't want to be his wife or their mother. I wanted to be like Billie Jean, rolling a two-seater with a silk scarf tied over my head, beholden to nobody, belonging to nobody but myself. I felt guilty, but also relieved, for finally being honest with myself. I marched right back to the den to announce my decision. But Monday Night Football had their attention. I realized I could show them better than I could tell them.

~~~~~

That Thursday evening, I sat on the floor of my closet, surrounded by the clothes I'd pulled from the rack, trying to find the difference between three pairs of cream slacks that looked exactly alike. I had no idea what I was going to do with most of this stuff—not too many people I knew could get in these fours and sixes. Suddenly, I felt a presence behind me. Not knowing if it was my husband or son, nor which I disliked it to be more, I folded the pants and did not turn around.

"Cilla, what's this all about?"

Sabre spoke and encircled me. I refused to look up at him.

"I told you the other day I was leaving. Wilma said I could stay with her as long as I needed to until we figure this thing out."

"Are you a bulldagger now? That's what you're doing? Is that why you cut your hair? Is that why you hadn't lain with me in years? 'Cause you riding down there and laying with Wilma in that dust over there at Carpenter's?"

I rolled my eyes. "Why would I want the gummy seconds and thirds after you done passed yourself around like your collection plates?" I sighed and added another pair of the slacks to the giveaway pile. "But that's neither here nor there, sir . . . It took me long enough, but I done retired my dog in this fight."

"Be forreal, Cilla—you're not."

He said this while reaching for me and then cupped my chin with his palm, a gesture that had varied meanings over the course of our marriage. In the early days, it meant he was going to kiss me. Later, it was purely for intimidation. I was having neither, so I jerked myself out of his grasp.

"No, Sabre, you're the one who's not! You got your boys. You got your hussies. You just won't have me anymore."

He grabbed the chair in front of my vanity and turned it so he could sit facing me. He did all this quietly, I guessed while searching for a new tack. When he spoke again, his voice came out all plaintive-like.

"I—I—feel like my world is falling apart."

"Now whose fault is that?"

"Cilla, I'm sorry, baby, what more can I say?"

"Sorry for goddamn what, Sabre? For having Kathareen all up in your office? For making me the laughingstock of town? For barging 'round here like a bully and letting these boys run amok? They haven't respected me since their sacks dropped."

"Now whose fault is that?"

"You bring up the DUIs but never the whys. You always undermine me! You didn't even make Emanuel keep seeing the damn therapist you know he needs."

"Cilla, it's a higher authority than any of those doctors. That's the one I let refer me and that goes for me and *my* house. You didn't give him time to heal from whatever happened before you began acting all suspicious with him. It's like you think he's guilty."

"I can't understand why you're not more curious about your son's extracurricular activities." I shook my head. "You know, I never left you because I was afraid of how other people were going to look at you. Tuh—I let you be the hero while I was your cross to bear. Well, I'm done with that story. Kathareen can have you. Matter of fact, she can have all six of you."

"Cilla, let me show you I can—"

"You can what?" I said. "Keep making me look like a damn fool?"

"Cilla, you act like we weren't in a marriage. Marriage goes both ways. You did things to me, too."

I thought about the look on his face on the day he came to bail me out. Artie hadn't put me in a cell, but I wanted to go in one when I saw how mad Sabre was. Of course, Artie them didn't know, but I sensed it bristling through his shirt. Come to think of it, I don't recall any hurt at all, and when we got home, all I saw was fury, a fury I never had the privilege of expressing. Had I been able to or brave enough to, maybe our relationship would not have come to this. But that was neither here nor there, so I said nothing and kept working.

"Look, Cilla, men of God shouldn't be begging nobody but Him."

"Oh, you can't beg for two minutes? After I done begged you for the last twenty years to be the man you claimed to be? After I been begging since July for you to fix this like you promised at the hospital? You wouldn't even consider sending him to Piney Woods like I suggested because you didn't want the scandal. But, hey, I always knew who you were when those robes was off. I know you better than you know yourself. But I'm done with all that now, and if you try to stop me, I'm going to air these secrets out one by one until your legacy is in total shambles. My shame been evident; yours is long overdue." I forced myself to calm my jagged breathing.

He sighed. "What are we going to tell our kids?"

"Whatever you want, Sabre, tell them whatever you want; you always have."

He said nothing, leaving me to work steadily through the pants and skirts until I had them all sorted. Maybe half an hour later, he reappeared.

"I don't want you at Wilma's," he said. "You don't have to stay with nobody when we got houses."

He handed me keys labeled Barnes, 1716, the Brickyard. I took them without question.

"Take the time you need to figure this out," he said, as if he were doing me a favor or giving me the permission I didn't need.

"I'm going to need some money, too."

I couldn't take my car. It would be after the first of the year before I could get my license reissued, but one step at a time, one step at a time.

～～～～

They put Ty in the ground on a cold, leaden Tuesday. It was cheaper than Sunday, and it wasn't like nobody was gone drive from Chicago or Milwaukee or even Memphis to come witness his sad, bare bones take their rest. I rode out to Heaven's Garden silently with Rev, but I stood with Bertha. I wore navy wool with a sable stole, one of the few things I would be keeping after my move. It was rumored that Ty had upwards toward ten kids. Only one, Lorraine's son, a painfully tall and slim and hapless-looking fellow, showed up. He sang "Near the Cross," in a beautiful baritone that seemed larger than his body, larger than this occasion. Ty's sister Glo, who was the closest to him, took it the hardest: Quincy had to hitch her up. Unfortunately, she didn't look long for this world herself, but no man knoweth their day nor hour. Rev was fiery, like he was getting practiced for a return to the pulpit. He likened Ty to the Prodigal Son, returned to glory in the Father's arms. I had to admit it was good, but it was all I could do not to scoff out loud. He sure was a piece of work.

DIAMOND

"I don't want to have my baby in the Reaping Season," I told Maggie.

I was almost twenty weeks then, and my bump didn't really show since I wore baggy clothes all the time. Maggie was at the window, peering through the blinds, as had been her habit of late. This couch had been my habit—first in the summer when I was so tired, and now in the fall because I was so bored. Since our escape to the coast, Maggie had been watching me like a hawk, and I couldn't go anywhere but school and church.

"A lot of stuff is going around," she said. "The devil is busy, and a lot of stuff is going around."

She was right, though. After the homecoming dance I didn't go to, Porky them were in a car crash. Champ was ejected from the car and killed instantly, and Marlon ended up paralyzed from the waist down, which basically meant football season was forfeited because the whole team was fucked-up over it. It really didn't matter because Rev. Winfrey was leaving his coaching position, like he'd left his ministry, and they had sent Emanuel to Dominion Academy with the white kids.

The day before Halloween, a hunter in Coahoma County found a heap of gnawed-up bones with dog tags that read Benny, Midas T. There was supposed to be an ongoing investigation. The only thing I had from our adventure was the Joker's notebook. Was this some of what the Winfreys had been trying to get out of me at the hospital? Did they think Wonder knew something about what happened to the Joker? Before we left, I remember him saying he was in trouble, but he never said why, and I got so caught up in the adventure that I had never thought to ask again. Was that why he had the notebook? No, Wonder wasn't the type to hurt anyone—especially not a harmless crackhead. I couldn't even fathom where their paths might have crossed. Then, with the rumors of another gang war, the city was debating canceling the Christmas parade again this year. I hated the staticky air, and I wished I could talk to Yancey, to make sure he was safe and tell him he was going to be an uncle.

"I don't want you to either, but this child is covered regardless! Amen!"

Her amen seemed definitive, made me feel less uneasy. I rubbed my belly. When Wonder announced that I was pregnant and said my mama's name, I knew he had a calling on him; I knew he came into my life to make me believe. And my faith remained strong even though I rarely got to see or talk to him anymore. So the worst part of it was that while all this stuff had been going down, I hadn't been able to talk to him about it or ease his mind at all. (They cut off the phone extension in his room, so we really had no privacy, and I even missed his birthday in September.) He didn't sing anymore in church, and it wasn't like I could talk to him there anyway. I snuck glances of him, all long in the face, in the back row with his daddy.

At least I could be grateful for the fact that if he was still at Dominion High, he most definitely would have been in that wreck with Porky them. Senior year so far had been a miserable bust—best year of my life, my ass. Nobody was in the mood to do anything but get out of Dominion on the first thing smoking after graduation. Most of them would be back in less than two years, but at least they would get to try. And me, I probably didn't even know how to drive anymore. Sometimes, in the midnight hour, I pulled the Joker's book from under my mattress and read it by lamplight. The most surprising thing was that it was so good even though it was a little sad. The stories were interesting, and he had included some simple and solid advice about life, like don't start nothing (like crack) that can't be finished and how wooden nickels don't spend. The words reminded me of the drinking, smoking, dice-rolling men I had always known from the White House. I couldn't throw it away.

PRISCILLA

The house on Barnes was in the Brickyard, on the other side of the river, far enough from Ashton that I'd never have to lay eyes on it if I didn't want to. Monday, I had Ivy take me to check the place out. On the drive over, his face was screwed up like he'd been sucking lemons.

"Are you really leaving us, Ma?"

"Baby, as long as I'm living, I'm your mama. I'm not leaving you at all. I'm looking out for myself."

"You can't do that at home with us? Who is going to cook and stuff?"

I laughed. "You're all men now and above your poor mother's station. Yall'll figure it out."

1716 was at the end of the block, where Barnes dead-ended at the intersection of Dorsey Road and firehouse #3. Keys at hand with Ivy close behind, I walked up the stone walkway of the small, yellow-sided bungalow. There was a white front door, a large window facing east, and enough yard to have a nice-sized garden. I opened the front door into the living room. It was older, probably from the early sixties, but the parquet floors were in good shape. The kitchen had yellow tiles and enough space for a table, but Sabre would have to replace these appliances ASAP.

I was giddy to find the house was something I could work with. Since the day I had announced my decision to leave, I had been wrestling with the idea of whether or not I was really going to move out. There was no doubt in my mind now. I could envision myself here, surrounded by only the things I loved and the people I wanted to be around, and although I had never in my life lived alone, I felt it would be good for me. I would put up a Christmas tree or not. I would have red wine in the living room with no bra on and my legs not crossed at the ankle. I would make chocolate chip cookies and eat them all myself, warm and sunk into some ice cream. I'd have days alone, at no one's beck and call, doing nothing but listening to the rain beat my roof.

We moved down the hall into the smaller of the bedrooms. Bright from the two big windows that met at the southwest corner, it offered a view of the backyard, where a lone lawn chair sat sideways on wet-looking Bermuda grass on the verge of being overgrown. It would be a perfect place for my piano. Maybe I'd give a few lessons again. This room had so much potential that I wanted to tell Ivy to leave me there to stay—yet I couldn't show that level of eagerness to my forlorn son.

"This will be my room," he said.

I said nothing but pulled Ivy close to comfort him with my embrace—because I couldn't comfort him with what he wanted me to say. I didn't need to tell him what he'd be learning soon enough, that he would have no room over here. I had done my part, and now they would have to stay over there at that fancy frat house with they daddy.

Over the next couple of days, while Manny was in school and Sabre at the shop or station, I made plans, and I made moves. I was taking almost none of the furniture with me, so after Ivy was done with his classes in the morning, we packed his truck with boxes and moved me out. No matter what went wrong, no matter how overwhelming, not even sleeping on an air mattress dampened my spirits, so ready was I for this new stage in my life. On a Saturday evening, Sabre supervised the installation of the appliances, and later, he and Ivy delivered the antique sofa that had been in my closet on Ashton. After a while, he sent Ivy to the car and kept trying to strike up a conversation with me. First, it was about Manny, but mainly he wanted to talk about us, which I flat-out wasn't going to discuss. Finally, he gone say, "You could at least stay at the house until you get this all done up the way you want."

Although I knew he thought he meant well, it almost set me off. I didn't want him to think he could dictate who I was and what I did anymore, whether he was financing it or not. This house was the least of what he owed me, *what I deserved*. If need be, we could let the courts work the money part out, but I would kick my feet up at Whitfield before I went back on Coon Hill with him. I said nothing in the moment, but my face must have told it all because he went, "But do it like you want to."

DIAMOND

Maggie and I were in her Chrysler, beeping outside the First Lady's new house. I sat in the back seat, thumbing through a *Seventeen* magazine without any focus at all. I didn't want to look up and see Wonder coming out of the door, but also, I was afraid of looking up and *not* seeing him come out. The day before, I had called him to remind him I was going to the doctor, but he was acting funny, and I could hardly get a word out of him. He didn't even get excited when I told him I had felt our baby moving for the first time (Maggie called it quickening). To be honest, he seemed totally uninterested, and I finally got sick of trying to talk to a blank wall and hung up on him. It didn't help that all day every day, I had nightmarish visions of him in his Dominion Academy kelly green polo, chasing white girls around the manicured grounds.

"I still can't believe she left him," Maggie said.

"Neither me," I said, rubbing the perfume card from the center of the magazine on my wrists and neck.

"You know what they say about what goes on behind closed doors."

"Most of that was going on in plain sight, Mama."

"You aint lying," she said. "She aint stepped back in the church since he left the pulpit either . . . Must be embarrassed."

After one last beep, the First Lady emerged, alone. My

heart felt like it had been poked with a nail; my bottom lip wiggled in wanting to frown. I forced it still. With an edge in my voice, I spoke.

"Why should she be embarrassed? What did she do wrong?"

Maggie didn't answer. What had the First Lady done but get cheated on? Why was that her fault? Both Maggie and I knew women who had been done way worse by scumbags with way less and stayed with them. What would I put up with to keep my family together? What would I do? I guessed all that would be clearer once my baby was more than just distant flutterings easily mistakable for gas. For now, my heart hurt in Wonder's absence. The First Lady yanked the door open; not only was it written all over her face, you could actually feel how cheerful she was now. She even seemed to limp less.

"How yall doing," she said, peeking over the headrest to include me in the greeting.

"We good," Maggie went for both of us. "How you, First Lady?"

"Maggie, girl, call me Priscilla or Cilla, please. I'm a lot of things, but what I aint is nobody's First Lady."

"Tuh," Maggie said. "I heard that."

"The boy had a project he's working on," said the First Lady. "They're shooting a video today at the school. Have you ever heard of something like that? They have them kids doing some of everything."

I didn't know if she made up this excuse to spare my feelings or to protect him; either way, I didn't believe her. I slammed the magazine shut and watched the dusty city fly by through the blur of my tears. Wonder's life didn't have to change if he didn't want it to. He could go to college and not be saddled with a kid. He got to be out at DA listening to the Backstreet Boys and swimming in Beckys, while I was stuck at the High, puking my guts up every second period (well, at least I wasn't sick anymore). In one stolen conversation, he confessed to me that he hated it out there. I'd sympathized with him, had believed he was miserable because I surely was. But now I wasn't so certain. *I need to know you will love me forever.* He had requested this of me, but it seemed he didn't actually want or need that. I couldn't imagine what I'd do if I suspected he was making the love we'd made on those steamy and adventurous nights with some other girl. I mean, he had been all in Trailerina's face when we were on the coast. It was weird because all that felt like another lifetime instead of just a couple of months ago. My body was on the verge of forgetting him.

Which made me consider possibilities I never had. I heard of girls, none I knew personally, sneaking up to Memphis to get abortions. Those that didn't have the money sat in hellacious bathwater and douched with Co-Cola. Or had somebody push them down the steps. It was the first time I had considered something of the sort for myself, and I was shocked at how detached I felt—as detached as Wonder seemed. I checked myself, leaned on my faith. Wonderboy had prophesied this baby and, by extension, our lives together; in that I had to take comfort—or else this was too hard. I was so deep in my thoughts that I didn't notice we were pulling into the parking lot of the Women's Clinic. I fake-smiled when I caught them both grinning over their seats at me.

"You ready, baby girl?"

I nodded.

Despite the fact that I had begun this thing a little under-weight, Dr. Wells said me and the baby were all good. The First Lady treated us to Borgononi's after the appointment. The restaurant was cool, dark, and almost empty because of the off hour. I had never been in there. Even though the place had tablecloths and wine, the food was kind of bland to me. Only the bread was good. I ate slice after slice, slathered in butter, while the First Lady and Maggie had too much wine and were laughing so loud the waiter kept scurrying over to officiate. But the manager, a rotund man with a thick mustache, was enam-ored with our table. He kept their wine coming, and he gave me a big slice of cheesecake for free. The First Lady was still giddy when we dropped her off. She leaned into the passenger-side window, pink from the wine.

"When I get everything all set up, I'll have yall over," she said.

Me and Maggie watched her stumble up the walkway, gig-gling to herself.

"You think she gone stick it out?"

"I hope so," I said, without really understanding why.

PRISCILLA

Wilma called to tell me they got a bed down at Carpenter's I would love. It must have arrived over the weekend because the store wasn't even open when I talked to her. The news couldn't have come a moment too soon, either; I had been alternat-ing between the air mattress and the bony antique sofa, and

I couldn't tell which was worse. Waking up on either had my back about ready to retire. As Wilma chatted, I pulled aside the curtain on the big living room window to see what kind of day it was: ashen, with the trees fluttering lightly but consistently in a breeze. I decided to ride down then instead of waiting for Ivy to take me.

I dressed in a pair of one of the boys' old sweats and retrieved my bike from the back porch. I drifted down the empty carport and pedaled the short distance to Dorsey. As I rode, I couldn't help but chuckle at Sabre's expense. Nothing in our entire relationship had ever shocked me like seeing his discomfort when he was no longer in control of every damn thing. Just two blocks south of Barnes, I could take the ramp down the riverbank to the trail, which was a straight shot to Carpenter's. I reached the trail in good time, but out of nowhere, I began to sweat feverishly, dampening the fleecy insides of the sweats in a way that felt slimy. I would have thought it just a random hot flash, but had my heart always raced like this during a flash? Did my hip scream from deep in the socket? A voice, petty, Godlike, thundered and echoed in my head:

You're making a damn fool of yourself. A damn fool.

"Shut up," I said, no, I spat. "Shut up."

But the voice ran on, telling me people were saying I lost my mind and that I was a terrible mother, and I would fail and run back to Sabre. Or the more unpleasant option of ending up in my hometown in one of my sisters' spare rooms. All because I hadn't done anything with my life beyond being some man's wife and baby-baker, and look at the nothing I had to show for it, not even the kids! Before I knew it, I had gone from smug and satisfied to a puddle on the ground, not knowing how I came to be there. A voice from behind startled me.

"You OK, ma'am?"

In front of me was a young couple who had probably been out strolling the trail. I don't know which one of them spoke, but the concern on their faces mortified me. I hadn't lived on Barnes a month, and here I was, already breaking down and in public, no less. But worse yet, as the young man helped me to my feet, some deep-hid yearning inside met and entangled with the musk of his strong body, a body that was not Sabre's. He held firmly to me, dusting me off, and I felt flushed, tickled, aroused, *shamed*. I dropped his forearm from my grip. The young lady handed me my bike.

"I'm fine," I said. "Thank yall."

They stayed a moment more to make sure, then they caught hands again and went toward the other end of the trail near the Canoe and Civic Center, while probably calling me a crazy old lady. I mounted the bike, rode the short distance to the highway, and quickly rolled across to Carpenter's. Wilma was waiting inside, wearing a cream sweater that made her seem even bustier. Her hug smelled of smoke and White Diamonds. I held on to her a long time; when we finally released each other, she asked me how it was going. I knew she was talking about the move, but I wanted to crack and blurt out everything that had been going on since the summer because the good Lord knew I needed to tell somebody. I recognized, however, that although I was at the end of my marriage, there would always be secrets to keep.

"It's an adjustment" was what I found to say.

Her eyes studied mine, as if she picked up on that need, but she didn't press the issue. "Craig and Jimmy went got this piece from an estate sale up in Harbor Town. When I saw it, I knew that it had come just for you, for your new place."

She was right—it was iron, king-sized, with beautiful scroll-work on the headboard and footboard and a bluish patina. They cut me a good deal on the bed and new mattresses, and I was all set. The frame was huge and heavy, so heavy that Craig and Ivy struggled to get it down the narrow hall to the bed-room. When it was all set up, I realized it was more suited for Ashton Court, and in this modest space, there would be room for little else, but I was thrilled because this was the sort of bed I had always wanted. In the days when I slept with Sabre, we lay in a big mahogany monstrosity passed down from his parents. Since he ran hot at night, he couldn't abide by extra pillows and whatnot, so I could make the bed with only sheets and a light blanket, and it pretty much resembled a convent. All the bedrooms did. I couldn't wait to layer my new bed with fuzzy, plush, silky things and stretch across it all by myself.

~~~~

I slept like a baby and woke early on Saturday for no reason at all, and after breakfast, I took my coffee to the backyard. I was only out there a minute when I recognized a familiar black Jag creeping up Dorsey. What the hell was Sabre doing? The car picked up speed and zoomed by, as if I wouldn't recognize the four corners of his head from any angle, at any speed. He had no reason sneaking around in these parts but to be in my busi-ness, and I didn't like the thought of that one bit. I went into the house, not wanting to admit to myself how the unexpected sight of him shook me. Had he been skulking about this whole time, and I was just noticing it? While I was washing the dishes, the doorbell rang. I hurried into the living room, peeked out of the window, and saw not Sabre but Manny. He was holding a huge box. I took a deep breath and a step back before opening the door, but still I stood in the large shadow he made.

"You didn't come to kill me, did you?"

The remark stopped him in his tracks.

"Ivy said this was yours," he said, and set the box down on the floor.

He appeared stricken. I had said the murder thing mostly as a joke, but the words had tumbled out bare-assed as the truth usually does. And he had been carrying a big-ass box. And honestly, I couldn't discount the fact that he or his daddy might indeed want me dead and in my grave. Women had been doused in battery acid for much, much less than leaving their husband. I told him to sit, while I went into the kitchen to gather myself. Rattled a pot. Ran some water. I ended up making him cocoa to justify being back there so long. When I set the mug in front of him, my shaky hand didn't go unnoticed.

"Baby, did you hurt that girl? Have you hurt others?"

"I wouldn't have no reason to hurt nobody, Ma. But I still don't remember much. I try to, but I can't."

He looked the same, but since the coast, his once-clear tone kept a rasp, and I wondered if it was permanent. It made him sound like an older man, with decades of smoking trapped in his throat. I realized I hadn't heard him sing since the summer and imagined he'd sound something like Bobby Womack.

"Emanuel, is it that you don't remember, or you don't want to remember?"

He sighed; his shoulders slumped. It all seemed so natural, but he had been acting all his life, and there was this thing he could not hide: the strange remoteness of his eyes. They were and were not mine.

"Is that why you left me? Because I messed up? Daddy said you're having a midlife crisis, and it's just a phase."

"I didn't leave you. I left the life I had with your daddy. We have irreconcilable differences, and we don't need to be together anymore. Do you understand?" He nodded and shrugged at the same time. "I was wrong not to talk to you boys about my decision, but that's my failure, not yours . . . But, baby, that doesn't take away from the fact that you need help."

"You think prison is help? That's what Daddy said."

"I don't want you in prison, but I can't let you be a danger to others . . . or yourself."

For a while he sat, dazed, with his cocoa, and I left him there for some invented work in the second bedroom, coming by every so often to take a glance at him. In those days before all this confusion, had Manny been trying to tell me something? I had refused to listen, to see. Had I stayed sober and diligent, would I have seen this coming? The Wooten girl was short and slender and hook-legged, tiny, even. Hurting her would've been like drowning kittens. I would have never thought my handsome, smart, talented, mannerable son would be out here throwing his weight around just 'cause. Surely many girls and even women would voluntarily appease his needs, whatever they were, just like they did his raggedy father.

That day with the Wootens, when he had passed by that girl's bitten face and smiled, I had seen him plain as a monster. Just as plain, now, he was subdued, humbled, almost sweet. Wherever he truly fell on that spectrum, I had helped create him, enable him. I was the one who had ushered the Wootens on out of the house, knowing good and well that boy could have done, likely had done, what they said. Ushered them out with prayer, no less. I had run from the situation in order to run from the guilt.

"You're going to be a father."

"I'm just not ready," he said.

"Well, you get ready."

He didn't seem to be the same—the edge that had been revealed was gone—but hell, I hadn't known who he really was in the first place. I refilled his cup with more warm cocoa, and I laid my hand on his head in a tender, motherly fashion. I would have rather cracked it open to see what made him who he was. Later, we went into the backyard, and he helped me rake leaves until this beeping sound kept interrupting. Finally, he unclipped a pager from his waistband and peered at it.

"It's Daddy," he said.

I was shocked at Sabre—pagers were for doctors and drug dealers, neither of which the boy was. I shook my head and kept working as he jogged into the house to phone his father. I didn't have the strength to even entertain why he had a pager, but I would eventually. I couldn't just check out completely. Had that been my intention?

"I gotta go," he said when he returned.

"What's this whole pager thing about?"

"Well, Dad thought I should have something in case of emergencies since I don't have a car anymore. But I'm earning it back."

He said this with a little lopsided grin that could charm anybody that didn't know better. But for me, it was almost as though he wanted me to pretend nothing had happened, that he was who I thought he was before. Sabre had decided to take him at face value. We hugged, and although it was a loving embrace, I felt coiled danger, his muscles with enough force to kill.

If he didn't remember, did that mean he was no longer the same boy that bit the Wooten girl in the face? Would that prevent him from doing the same thing to someone else? Or would his depravities, unchecked, quietly evolve into something more fearsome? He would be a terror on a college campus, an absolute terror. And one where he was again a star? Could he be a danger to Diamond, poor orphan Diamond, who thought his shit didn't stink? Or to their child? Was I willing to take that chance with a baby's life? Or anybody else's?

I went inside and fixed a double shot, despite the fact it was well before noon. Poured it down and instantly, the tightness in my head fell loose. After a while, I began unpacking the box Emanuel had brought. It contained random stuff—a shawl, house shoes, old Sunday school books—things Sabre could've kept or trashed. Seemed like he had gotten used to the idea of me being gone and decided to help clear me out for good. Tuh! At the bottom was an accident: the box from Emanuel's room that I hadn't been able to find. Seeing it caused all the questions that lingered in the back of my mind and the fears I'd tucked behind my heart to rush into my throat, as if to force out what I had kept myself from fully considering. I had no choice in that moment but see what there was to see.

DIAMOND

Something about being on this loud, squirmy school bus made me feel sick. I tried to tune my environment out but couldn't. Even though it was the week before Thanksgiving, and the weather was cool, the bus was intensely hot and smelled musty with a hint of something unidentifiable but very unpleasant. It was a relief that my stop was next, and I stood, just as Mr. Liner was braking. The bus squealed and lurched, and me right along with it. Some kid caught my arm, and I had ahold of a seat; between us, I was able to stay on my feet. I thanked whoever it was, then frantically reached beneath the bookbag that I carried in front (like all the pregnant girls did) and placed my palm on my belly. *It's OK. We're OK.* Carefully, I made my way through the maze of knees and feet to exit. Ignored Mr. Liner, who took his job way too seriously, yelling about some bus safety. As I walked home, I held myself and chanted, just under my breath: "It's OK. We're OK. It's OK. We're OK." It kept me going like NamMyohoRengeKyo. Then, I remembered that after band practice, Bunny was taking me to Coon Hill so I could stare at the Winfreys' door. Well, she said she might.

All the time she was like, "You're so pretty, friend. You can do way better. Just focus on your baby."

But how could she say that? And who asked her anyway?

How could I separate thoughts of my baby from the one who gifted her to me? Had she not seen how beautiful Wonderboy was? How sweet? Surely, Bunny had never felt anybody uncoil their light in her body. At home, I locked the glass storm door but kept the wooden one open, so I could watch out for her. The house was clean, and I had done all my work either in class or study hall. That was the only positive thing about this year: I was going to have a good GPA.

There was no show I wanted to watch, no activity I wanted to participate in but loving him, so I waited with a long face for my friend to arrive. But five came and went, and I paced the living room, knowing band practice had to be long over, but still, Miss Bunny didn't show. We only had a few minutes to get all the way to Ashton before she had to be back home for good. Instinct told me to walk around to her house, despite the sun setting like it was late for an event. Sure enough, her little dusty Corolla was in the driveway. I ran the three blocks home to call and snap on her, but when I got there, I found myself dialing Wonderboy instead. A manly voice answered that was not his or the Reverend's.

"Emanuel," is the only word I could get out.

"He's not in."

I slammed the phone down in whoever's face. Went to the refrigerator and dumped the last of the spaghetti out of the Country Crock tub, smothered it with cheese, heated it, and gobbled it down, knowing I would probably be burping all night. I tried not to think about where he was and what or who he might be doing. I had just washed the dishes when the phone rang. The caller ID said Winfrey, Sabre J., but when I snatched up the receiver, it wasn't Wonderboy. It was the First Lady. My heart sank when I heard her voice.

"He don't love me, do he?"

"I'm his mama, and I don't know anything about him," she said. "You don't either, and you'll never be able to. You're fooling yourself if you think otherwise."

The words were harsh and, though put gently, felt like an I-told-you-so.

"What will I do?"

"You will worry about loving you and your baby. Then you're going to do you. That's what you're going to do. Go to college. Go on trips. Make friends. Live a life. And never, ever, ever will you try to lose or find yourself in somebody else because you'll be lost in the desert if you do."

But who was she to think she knew what was right for me? She didn't know nothing about love but how to get her man took.

"With all due respect, First Lady, I don't think that will work for me."

And then her voice had that tone I remembered from the hospital, and she was telling me to tell Maggie to bring me by the house on Sunday.

~~~~

In the cafeteria that Friday, we had fish, and I almost broke down because I would have gladly given Wonder my fish if he were there to ask. But what was worse, as I was taking my first hot-sauced-juicy bite, Shanice and one of her girls stank-walked over to the table behind me and Bunny. I was still sort of mad at Bunny for not coming by the other day, but she didn't seem to care, just shrugged like she always did. I hadn't even bothered to tell her what the First Lady said because I knew she was going to agree with her. As I was thinking this, Shanice began loud-talking.

"When the last time you seen your baby daddy, girl? I heard he got the jungle fever out there at DA."

The bite in my mouth turned sawdust dry. I started to spit it into my napkin before I said something but I went ahead and swallowed because I didn't want to waste the bite. I was about to turn around and confront her when Bunny shook her head.

"Ignore her, girl," she whispered. "She don't know nothing, and if she did, what could you do about it?"

I sighed and side-eyed Bunny—if she was just that smart, she should have figured out how to get rid of that mustache by now. But, whatever, I followed her advice and said nothing, and they moved on when I didn't take the bait. It wasn't like I was going to fight Shanice or anything. She probably wanted to try to make me lose my baby because she was jealous. Still, the situation ruined my appetite. I wrapped my fish sandwich in napkins, so I could sneak and eat it in World History when I got hungry again. As I was doing just that, Mrs. Kathareen, everybody's favorite home-wrecker, crossed my mind. Why were men willing to risk for her, to work for her? I needed to know the source of her power, and I needed to grab some for myself. There were other good-looking and fine women in church, but none carried her heft. She wasn't just a head-turner; she was a neck-breaker, a whiplash. Not even the First

Lady's gray eyes were that powerful. I knew Mrs. Kat did roots for some of the women in church for the shit God didn't handle. Maybe she could do that for me. Because out of all the praying I'd done for Wonder, he had yet to be mine again, and I was losing patience.

The next day, while Maggie slept, I walked the three blocks to Mrs. Kathareen's house. When she opened the door, she seemed surprised but not upset or anything. She wore a red silk kimono and some kind of musky sweetness that overwhelmed me when she snatched me into a hug and locked the door behind us. I guess my expression concerned her.

"You OK, Diamond? Maggie alright?"

"Nothing's wrong, Mrs. Kathareen—it's me—I'm the one that needs to talk to you—in private if we can."

"Let's go into my office."

Inside smelled of that good Saturday-morning cleaning plus faintly of bacon. I couldn't help but sneak glances at her magnificent form and the sure way she moved. Her waist cinched way in, but her breasts, hips, behind, all spilled out in a cornucopia of body—almost like she was a different species from me. She didn't need a root, a spell, or nothing else to catch anybody, and even for me, being so close to her in that thin slip of kimono was tingly and uncomfortable in strange places. I couldn't believe a man would leave her to wait or worry unless he had to die like her husband. In her kitchen, she directed me to sit at the table and offered me food. I told her I had just eaten, and she came to sit across from me and nodded expectantly.

"What can I do for you, Diamond?"

But when I opened my mouth, nothing came out. I had been going to the Seals as long as I had been with Maggie, and Mrs. Kathareen had been there at least since then, but never had I really looked her in the face. Across her kitchen table, I found she actually looked like a cat, like a brown, silky cat. She was unbothered like cats were. As I sat before her glory, slumped and dejected like I was, and with this particular request, I grew more and more inflamed.

"I—I know you help people," I stammered. "Like with roots."

She tilted her head but said nothing, stared at my struggle to put thoughts to words.

"I lost my mama, I lost my sister and brother, I lost Cordelia. I can't . . . I can't."

I stopped. She scooted into the seat closer to me, brushing me with her silk, her scent. "You can tell me, honey."

So I blurted: "I want you to make Wonderboy marry me and love only me for the rest of his life."

She sighed, and there was such a long pause afterwards that I knew I had skipped down here and embarrassed myself in front of this lady for absolutely nothing.

"That's not the sort of thing I do, Diamond. And besides, you never want to approach love that way. People—"

"But, Mrs. Kathareen, you don't understand—I want him! I want his *mind*."

"You hear what you asking for? You want a zombie? A Mr. Frankenstein?"

"No, not that but like—"

"How old are you, Diamond?"

"I will be eighteen soon." My voice faltered into nothing.

I knew when adults asked this question, you probably weren't going to get the answer you wanted.

"Seventeen with many years ahead of you. Do you understand there's a whole huge world out there and you've experienced none of it, yet you want to throw yourself at the first person you think you're in love with? There are lovers more tender, more attentive and romantic, more beautiful, more broad, more everything—and less of all the shit they don't need to be—who will gladly worship you."

I whined, "But I don't want them."

Her expression was serious as a heart attack. "Girl, you don't know enough to know what you don't want. You haven't even gotten to know yourself. Hell, you might not even want him in a year, let alone forever." She lowered her tone. "Please, Diamond, listen to me. Graduate, and get you and your baby out of Dominion, and give yourself a chance to do something that fulfills you. And really live, baby girl. You aint even lived enough to want to bind yourself to someone for the rest of your time on Earth."

Mrs. Kathareen's unwanted lecture reminded me so much of the First Lady's unwanted lecture that I wanted to mention it in a cheeky little way. But her face was so sincere, and I was still a sweet person, despite all of these disappointments.

"Diamond, you'll never have to force real love. Matter of fact, real love is so special and so strong it cannot be forced."

I stood to leave, ignoring the fact that her last statement added up to the perfect sum. She really was no help at all.

"But you have power," I said.

"What do you mean?"

"You have power over men—that other women don't have."

"Nooooo, baby girl, my only power is that I won't give my power away."

Whatever that meant.

"Before you go." She flitted away and around, returned and pushed into my hands a brown paper sack.

"Thank you for talking with me, Mrs. Kathareen. Please don't tell Maggie."

"Understood," she said.

On my way home, I peeked into the bag. There were two pound-cake muffins wrapped in foil, a mini bottle of Florida water, and a small, solid packet of herbs, for what I didn't know. While I was in the bag, I decided to try one of the muffins, and honestly, it was kinda dry. I walked into the house a little less than an hour after I'd left and went to check on Maggie, and she was still asleep. I was out of ideas, out of energy, out of everything, but I mustered the strength to get the chocolate milk (which I didn't like until I got pregnant) and make it back to the couch to eat the other muffin. I tried not to think about what the First Lady wanted to talk to me about. Of course, it could be good, like a quick wedding for now and a huge one after he goes to the NFL. By the second ceremony, I will have found Cricket and Popeye, and it could be a celebration forreal. (But for now, I would gladly give anything for another of our sun-soaked afternoons in the Canoe.) Somehow, something told me none of that would be the case. I found myself pushing my two fingers in my mouth like Popeye would to make himself feel better.

9

PRISCILLA

Diamond arrived swaddled in Emanuel's hoodie, had it tied so tight around her head that it was symbolic for how he had ahold of her mind. The thing was, he wasn't studying her in the least. As I was locking the door, I saw her plop down on the sofa, and I saw the moment her narrow behind met one of the couch's bones, and she popped back up. But you don't plop down on other folks' furniture for the same reason you don't pet strange dogs. Of course, some of life's lessons will only be purchased with pain and blood. I stood over her like I was a waiter or something.

"How are you feeling, Diamond? You want some grits? I have sausage and eggs, too, if you're hungry."

She shook her head; I felt her wretchedness in the pit of me, felt the heartbreak of the instant your hopes are dashed against stone.

"Diamond, I know you think you love Emanuel, but he is no good for anyone, I promise you. No good for you or a baby. Leave him be and do what you need to do for yourself. You should have the chance to make a life for yourself. I want to extend to you the same opportunity he has to go to school. Between Rev and financial aid, we can put you through college. If you have a tech program you like, we can pay for you to do

203

that. If you want to go away to school, I'll keep the baby for you right here, and if Maggie wants to help, she can."

"Oh, so that's what this is about. Yall want to steal my baby. You don't think I'm good enough to have the first Winfrey grandchild."

"No, no, no, Diamond. That's not what this is at all. I'm worried about you and your safety, the safety of the baby."

"What do you mean? Wonderboy would not hurt a fly."

"He might not hurt a fly, but he would hurt people, Diamond, and I don't want one of them to be you, and I definitely don't want one of them to be the baby."

"How can you say these things about your own son? Your own flesh and blood? Pardon my language, First Lady, but that's fucked up."

Here she rubbed her belly, as if to show me and reassure her child that she'd never be like me. I went to the second room for the box, returned, and set it on her lap.

"I hate to have to do this to you but open it. See what I'm talking about."

"What's this?"

I opened the lid, watched her eyes buck as she found what I had discovered. The envelopes had held panties in all colors and sizes. Small, red, gnarled ones of cheap polyester lace. A blue-striped thong, fit for a large bottom. Pink boy shorts. Some very low-rise lime green ones that I couldn't imagine flattering anybody. A purple bikini.

"The box is his, Emanuel's."

"Why would he have these? Whose are they?"

"Your guess is good as mine about why he has them, but I'm guessing at least one pair belongs to Caticia Wooten."

"Caticia Wooten?" The girl looked taken aback. "What about her?"

"You know her? The day you and Emanuel decided to run away together, her daddy brought her over to the house; he was about to go to the police because she said Emanuel assaulted her. That's why he ran away. He didn't want the consequences."

"I don't believe you. None of this makes any sense at all. We lost our virginity to each other."

She had her hand in the box again, was pulling out something. She gasped.

"I made this bracelet for my brother, Yancey, when we were kids," she said. "He was wearing it the last time I saw him. Wonderboy was with me, but how—how would he get this bracelet? Why would Wonder have this?"

Lord, I didn't know for sure, but whatever reason he had it, it didn't bode well for Brother Yancey. I was afraid to say what I thought aloud, could only hope the bracelet was some kind of accident.

"Have you seen Yancey lately?"

"We haven't had regular contact since we were kids— I usually just have to catch him here and there. He had problems he was working on."

Her voice trailed away, but she continued to finger the bracelet.

I hated to push her, but I had to. "When yall left, did he

tell you anything about what had been going on in the last couple of days? Did he tell you anything about the Joker? Or a notebook?"

Diamond looked at me. "I saw the notebook. I just don't know where it went."

She went silent again, but on her face, I could practically see her reckoning, then awareness, then panic, then her recomposing herself. Her voice came out tiny, as if volume would crush the composure she'd tried to build: "Can we go to the police? And can we like file a missing persons on Yancey?"

"You mean go to his daddy friends?" I said. "And tell them he, a teenaged boy, had a bunch of girls' draws? They aint gone do nothing but clap him on the back and congratulate him. As for the bracelet, it's going to be a hard sell. You yourself said your brother was a rolling stone."

"What can we do then?"

"Is there anything else you remember?"

"Before we left, he said something like I might hear some things about him and made me promise I would still love him, no matter what, but I swear to God he didn't explain nothing. I just hope my brother is alright. That's the only family I have, maybe, except Maggie. Wonder knows that; no, no, no, he would never hurt him."

The girl began to wail, which swelled into wild, jagged weeping. I had made a huge mistake asking her here, in telling her this. I had no one I could trust to keep it secret, and I really wasn't keen on putting my son out there for the scrutiny of others with no real facts, but I shouldn't have brought her into this.

"We don't know anything's wrong yet, Diamond. Let's see if we can find him first."

She cried herself into a puddle. I wanted to hug her, to comfort her, but part of me considered this her fault, too. She stood suddenly, then it appeared she was trying to go in two directions at the same time. Unsuccessful, she doubled over and heaved her breakfast all over my coffee table. I cursed, rushed into the kitchen for something to clean with.

"Go take care of yourself," I told her. "The bathroom is the first door to the right."

She stayed in there a long time, running water and flushing. She emerged wiping her mouth with a paper towel. I finished cleaning the mess and rose to take the trash to the kitchen.

"Why don't you come to church now? You must not believe in God no more?"

The question caught me by surprise, and I had to reach to find an answer. "Of course I believe in God. I no longer believe in the Seals."

"I need money," she said abruptly. "Two hundred dollars."

Her request and the seriousness in her face stunned me. I went for my checkbook. "I don't have that much cash hanging around."

"I can't do anything with that," she said. "I don't have an ID. You have to get me cash."

"You don't have a license?" I said, sort of flippantly.

"Do *you* have one?" she asked, just as flippantly back.

DIAMOND

Maggie's horn beeping outside was a sweet relief, and I hopped to my feet to get out of that house. The First Lady had been in another room for some time, and just as I was at the front door, her head poked out from the hallway.

"Give me a second," she said.

But I kept going. By the time I was halfway down the walk, she was on the front porch, tugging a wobbly suitcase behind her, moving fast, too, almost like she had chased me out. I got into the car and turned the radio on and up. Maggie adjusted it, was rolling down the window as the First Lady deposited the bag into the back seat. She leaned in it to speak.

"These are the clothes I've been meaning to give you. Remember what I told you about the dry-clean-only ones."

She had said nothing at all about dry cleaning clothes, so this I knew was her way of reminding me to keep what we had discussed on the hush. Which I heard as *don't betray him*, which I knew meant *don't betray us*. Which made me strongly doubt, as I buckled myself in, that she would do anything at all. Why would she—especially if it meant Wonderboy might go to jail forever?

"How was service?"

Maggie rolled her eyes and shook her head. "Youth Sunday and half the youth didn't show up 'cause they parents didn't. Nobody don't want to hear Espy's mushmouth gobble. We need him out of there like yesterday. Any word on Rev's return?"

"I don't know nothing about that, girl," said the First Lady. "You'd do better asking Kathareen."

"Well, you still my First Lady, and I still got hope for yall marriage," said Maggie. "How'd your little girl talk go?"

Me and the First Lady automatically glanced at each other then quickly away.

"She gone be good," the First Lady said to Maggie. "We all gone be fine."

After we drove off, I thought Maggie would be on me about what the First Lady and I had discussed, but she chatted about church. She said the Reverend and Wonderboy had stood at altar call and rededicated their lives to God; the sound of his name caused a sourness to pucker my mouth. It didn't help that I kept getting whiffs of vomit from the hoodie. I couldn't wait to rip it off and toss it in the nearest dumpster. Maggie went into the kitchen to heat dinner, and I headed right through to the bathroom to get the tub started. It wasn't until I heard the heat shift on that I realized the uncomfortable chill that had set in my bones. I quickly undressed and slid into the hot water.

As usual, my hand went right to my belly, but this time, I snatched that hand away. The thing felt rigid and bad and wrong and gross. Like that time at the Sunflower when Ms. Yvonne sent us a box of Twinkies and Cricket's had this weird little knot of Twinkie flesh on one end, and she screamed and refused to eat it. Mama had explained to her that there was nothing wrong with it; it was simply a manufacturing error. And Yancey snatched the cake from where Cricket tossed it and swallowed it down grinning, and she wouldn't let him sit near her for weeks. She claimed he'd grow a knot like the Twinkie. The memory made me laugh, but it also made me sad. My sweet, sad brother could be dead in a ditch like the Joker and here I was carrying the manufacturing error of his killer. I had to hate this thing inside me if I hated Wonderboy. Maybe after I gave birth, I would lend the baby to the First Lady and then go off and live my life and forget I'd had a kid. Maybe that's what my mama had done. Before I knew it, I was sobbing, and Maggie was knocking.

"I'm alright. I'll be out in a minute."

I was like those women on the Lifetime movies me and Maggie watched. I was stupid, so damn stupid. Like them, I had been so confident in love but so wrong. Would I always be like them? At risk for this sort of pain and confusion. After I was done washing and dressing, we sat down to eat. Maggie had made pinto beans, but the roast was a dried-out mess, so she had run out and bought a box of chicken. I was starving, but my body was acting like it wasn't going to cooperate with eating.

"I figured what the First Lady said might upset you. Do you want to talk about it?"

"You know what she said?"

"We talked. I thought it might be good for you to take her up on that offer. Your baby will be in good hands. I'll have her when the First Lady needs a rest, and when you come home for your college breaks, yall can bond . . . But no one's trying to force you to do anything, baby girl. It's completely your choice, and I'm here for you regardless."

"Oh, it's not 'cause you tired of me and don't want a baby

screaming on top of that?" I shoved a drumstick in my mouth, as if that would soften the statement.

"Don't, Diamond," she said. "Just don't."

Sadness was on her face or disappointment maybe in how I had turned out.

"Can I wash dishes and lay down? I don't feel so good."

"Go," she said, "I got this."

I grabbed the phone and called Wonderboy from the bathroom. I desperately needed to talk to him. My hello was meek. Theirs wasn't.

"Who is this?"

Immediately I hung up, upset by the roughness in the tone. The exchange was so brief, and they were brothers, so of course, they might sound alike, but something told me it was Wonder who had answered. Before I could sink too much into the miserable, ugly feeling that had begun when the First Lady started talking that morning, I decided to go apologize to Maggie, the one person I knew had me. She was still at the table; the way she was staring into space made me feel even worse.

"Can I have some sugar?"

She hmmphed me, but she aimed her cheek up for me to graze. Maggie was built solid, strong legs and shoulders, a beautiful back, but she *was* fifty-six, and I didn't know if I was imagining things, but her skin seemed fragile to me, papery even, like layers might have come off with my kiss. Here I was taking my frustrations out on her, and if something happened to her, I'd be sick, maybe even jump off the bridge or something.

~~~~~~

The First Lady didn't call me Monday or Tuesday, and by Wednesday, I had concluded she had no intention whatsoever of doing any sort of investigation. The sole purpose of that little meeting was to try to keep me away from Wonderboy. But that was more than OK, I was cool on him anyway. Besides, I had spent the days using my head for more than just a hat rack. I hatched a plan myself, and it all started with her money. The day before Thanksgiving, school set us free at noon, and I collected my bag lunch and rolled out with Bunny.

We went to the Xpress Mart, so I could fill her tank, and I promised her a dozen hot tamales from Mr. Hicks after. First, we drove to the only house I had known Yancey to live in, but it was boarded up. An old girlfriend we caught outside DeSoto Projects hadn't seen him but told us to tell him to holler at her when we found him. Last, we came up Yazoo, toward where the council met. I could see from a couple of blocks down that there were buckets and milk crates and men; my heart beat faster in anticipation of laying hands on my brother. But I saw as we got closer that Yancey was not one of them. I recognized the dude who had called me pretty, and I asked Bunny to pull over. When I got out, he stood and kind of leaned to the side, as if he were trying to place me.

"There she go," he said. "There her go."

He was short but stocky, a wide smile full of big teeth.

"Do you remember me?"

"Of course, I 'member you—a man don't usually forget a face this pretty. You Smoke baby tender."

"Yes," I practically screamed. "How you been? Have you seen him lately?"

The man cupped his chin with his fingers, stared upwards and off to one side like he was searching a corner of his brain. "Naw, matter of fact, I hadn't seen him since 'round 'bout that time I seent you. Oh, yeah, not since he left here with ol dude in a truck one morning." He stopped talking and looked around the council.

"Any of yall seen skinny Smoke lately?"

A chorus of nahs and stares came from the men. The ground and my insides shook in a way that they had to no-tice, adding a layer of self-consciousness to my terror. My mind spun; the tears flew, automatic.

"Ah, don't do that, baby girl. Your brother alright. When I see him, I'll tell him to call you. Matter fact, Imma make him call you."

I handed the man a ten-dollar bill and thanked him. Started toward Bunny's car.

"What he say?" she asked.

"None of them have seen him."

She slipped her arm around me and gave me a squeeze. "Friend, it's gone be OK; he gone be alright."

Caticia Wooten crossed my mind, what the First Lady said Wonderboy did to her. I thought about her daddy, too, how he used to be up at the school every time she tried out for some-thing. "Can I ask you something, Bunny?"

"Go head," she said, adjusting the radio.

"Even from the beginning you didn't like Wonderboy. Why? Do you know something about him I don't? Did he do something to you?"

"Why did you ask me that? What does this have to do with your brother?"

"I asked you because I want to know. I been thinking a lot lately—since he been doing me wrong—how you never liked him in the first place."

"It's just something about him," she said.

"He don't look good to you?"

"I mean I guess, but they always say the devil was good-looking, too."

What she said stunned me. *"You think Wonderboy's the devil?"*

"Girl, I don't think nothing about him at all. I think I'm ready for my hot tamales, though."

I got her some and some for home, too. Bunny came in with me, and we sat at the table with Maggie and ate the hot tamales with crackers and ice-cold Cokes out of the refrigerator, laughed with them, but my mind was somewhere else altogether. After Maggie went to work, I called to tell the First Lady what I had discovered. But she wanted to report to me that the bracelet was gone and so was one of the pairs of panties. I was fiddling with the bracelet on my wrist as I told her I didn't know nothing about it. We could all be some lying bitches if that was how she wanted to play it. For some reason, I thought of Caticia again, how her daddy would always be there.

10

It was the Monday after Thanksgiving. Jimmy Wooten loosened his bow tie and tossed his cummerbund over his shoulder. In his right hand, he gripped the tightly twisted paper bag holding his fifth of gin. As he approached the house, he saw how overgrown the yard had become, the way the overfilled trash can needed to be pushed to the curb. He just had so much on his mind lately that he hadn't been able to keep all he had to do straight. He paused to unwind the bag and take a long, needed swig from his bottle. He capped the bottle and resumed his walk to his front door.

"Get it together or get help, Jimmy Dell," he could hear Marsha saying.

He was forever telling her they needed to move to where there were more opportunities than riding up to the boat. The Delta was dead for Black folk, but she insisted on staying to be close to her mama. He mounted the porch stairs, lifted the lid of and swept the mailbox, found a circular from the dollar store and a manila envelope, which he teased out from behind it. JIMMY WOOTEN, it read in a tiny, even handwriting he didn't recognize—like a mouse had wrote the shit. No return address or postage; the envelope had been placed in the box, not mailed to it. He squeezed, felt something soft and bulky.

Confused, he set the bottle on the porch chair and ripped open the envelope. Panties were inside, ones that had the leg stretched out of shape. Were these Tish's? Did that boy do this? His blood pressure skyrocketed to block out the picture of his daughter, terrified and trembling beneath Winfrey; he broke out into a sweat that wouldn't fall, just stood there still enough to make him uncomfortable. If he were a man with any more weight, a few ounces more muscle, he would have popped out of the white tuxedo shirt and saggy black Dickies like the Hulk. He stuffed the draws and the envelope into his pocket and burst into the door of his house. Tish jumped off the couch, dropped the GED book she had been studying. She had really straightened up, said she wanted to be a lawyer now. Marsha warned the girl to set her sights lower, like a paralegal or a court reporter, but Jimmy had staunchly and stubbornly told the girl she could do whatever she put her mind to.

"Good," he said to himself.

Because he would probably need her to get him off after he killed this boy.

"Daddy, who are you talking to? What's wrong?"

He said nothing to her, pounded down the hall toward his and Marsha's bedroom, and reached into the side table for his pistol. Tish had followed, gaped at him when he turned around with the gun.

"No, Daddy. Where you going with that?"

"Tish, I need you to go in that living room, keep your mouth closed, and stay in a child's place. And tend to your brother and sister when they get home."

Jimmy jumped right back into his car. He knew the Winfrey boy was at Dominion Academy because he'd been in the newspaper every week since the 3A football finals were coming up.

He snatched the gin bottle and headed out to their field house. It was up 61, on the outskirts of town, on the way to work, so he really didn't even want to go, but he knew he had to. When he got there, the gates were locked up, but the parking lot was open. It was after 4:30; they should be coming out of there soon, right? During the spell he waited, he wondered why, after all these months, did this boy want to test him in this way? Who did he think he was? Taking his daughter, snatching her, disposing of her, and then taunting . . . Naw, hell, naw.

He had been waiting maybe fifteen minutes when a pink Bug with eyelashes on the lights crunched into the lot right beside him. The windows were down. A blond-headed girl with a bad tanning bed habit popped gum and bumped Tupac. Jimmy wanted to drive and repark but couldn't think of a way to do so without being any more conspicuous than he already was. At least there was the murky cover of sunset, and the girl's preoccupation with looking at herself in her visor mirror. Just as he had decided to go home, another car and another showed up. The football players began emerging from the building in clots.

At last, the Winfrey boy appeared, flanked by two buff Biffs with Lego man haircuts that they flipped off their foreheads. He dapped them both and got in the little pink Bug with the blond-headed girl. Jimmy watched them tongue wrestle for a moment before she drove off. This boy here was shonuff wild and delusional, thinking he could be out here playing with these rich and pink pussies like it was nothing. It might be the year 2000, but it was still Mississippi. Jimmy sipped his gin and shook his head as he trailed the little pink Bug from one car behind. They made a stop for fast food and rolled into the parking lot behind the church's restaurant. Jimmy stayed back a ways, behind a bush that hung over the curb. He wanted to rap the butt of his .38 on the quickly fogging windows of that ugly, stupid Bug, yank that boy out of there, pistol-whip him, and while he begged for his sorry life, shoot him in the johnson. Even if he didn't die, he'd want to every single day of the miserable-ass rest of his life. But if he did that, he'd have to kill this blond child, and Jimmy simply wasn't that kind of man, so he drove home to face the questioning eyes of his family.

~~~~~

On Saturday, he woke early and in the twilight of his bedroom, stared at his beautiful wife. She was a bad mama jama they used to call Cupcake in the day; sometimes he still did. He had been elated when she chose him and kept choosing him, knowing she could have rightfully had a pampered life with some other man. But she wanted him: brown, plain Jimmy Dell Wooten from the backwoods of Mattson. She *deserved* a man that would avenge his family; his kids deserved a father that would protect them. He tucked the feathery hair that peeked from underneath her headscarf, so it wouldn't ruin the back of her wrap when she combed it down. The gesture woke her. How sweet she was, softened by sleep like this. He bent down and kissed her; a long, cold tear he couldn't trace or stop had fallen from his face to hers. She came completely into consciousness at once, rose quickly.

"What's the matter, Jimmy Dell?"

"Nothing, baby," he said. "You were just so beautiful lying there."

"There is something wrong, Jimmy Dell. After all this time, I know when you bothered."

"I'm not bothered, baby, and there's nothing wrong."

He hated lying to her, hated shutting her out of his thoughts, but he didn't want her opinion on the matter. Nor did he want her radar on, so he kissed her again, and she kissed him with full and sweet fervor, with a small side of nasty. He could feel himself grow erect. He knew he didn't have time for this, but considering his plans for the day, it might be the last time, so he raised her nightgown and plunged into his willing wife, moving within her as if he were soon to be off to war. He hated to be so rough with how he held her mouth, but he did not want her to wake the children. Afterwards, she went right to sleep. He washed up and dressed in a gray sweatsuit, over which he donned a kelly green windbreaker he'd taken from the lost and found at work. He had snuck past the girls' bedroom to get to the bathroom, but Tish waited for him in the living room.

"Daddy, where are you going in that?" she said, pointing at the telltale green windbreaker.

He didn't want to cry in front of her, but the idea that he had let her down had rocked him for all these months, so that he had to briefly turn away from her to catch an errant tear with his knuckle.

"Daddy, what if something happens to you? What we gone do? Daddy, please. I love you. I'm sorry. I'm sorry."

If she started the waterworks, he would never be able to leave her there crying, and the mission would be a bust.

"Quit it, Tish. Go back to bed, and don't worry your mama."

~~~~~

Either the wide receiver didn't have enough hustle to get to the ball, or the quarterback put too much mustard on the pass—that part was up to interpretation—either way, the ball was intercepted in the last seconds, failing to tie the game and go to overtime. Either way, Jimmy thoroughly enjoyed witnessing the loss. He sipped his gin while he trailed the Jaguar that trailed the Bug that trailed the bus of sad white boys and one little nigger that was about to lose his life.

At the buffet at the Western Sizzlin, Jimmy enjoyed prime rib and baked potato with real bacon and chives on DA's tab and ear-hustled in plain sight.

"Son, how many times do I have to tell you that if you playing catch-up the whole game, you done already lost? You out there panicking 'cause yall were behind all night and scared! Rather you stand ten toes down in the pocket and get a good pass off and take that lick than flail around running like a sissy and get picked off. You gotta think and make good decisions. Now granted those white boys aint Demarcus or Marlon, but still, you're the star, and unfortunately, you gone be sprinting tomorrow morning before church."

"Yes, sir," the boy said.

Shit, chuckled Jimmy, *no wonder, no wonder*.

It wasn't until around six that the caravan arrived at the DA field house. Jimmy waited patiently as the boys filed silently out of the building. The Winfrey boy walked toward the Jaguar, where his father leaned with his arms crossed.

~~~~~

Jimmy Wooten was circling through Coon Hill when he saw the pink Bug pull onto Ashton Court. *These kids was natchy bold!* The boy came out and hopped in, and when they were off, Jimmy was in tow. From afar, he copied their winding route out of town into Rena Lara, where some of the long-money, old-money Delta folk holed themselves. The mansion sat amidst a corolla of crop fields. Boasted a large pond with a paddleboat and maybe twenty acres of woods to the rear of it. The night was haunting and spectacular. A cobwebby gray sky blurring the sickle moon. Black skeleton tree fingers reaching up. Cold that belonged to February, not December. A perfect night for the Reaper to prowl, a beautiful night to die, Jimmy thought, as he eased onto the narrow shoulder, too cautious to get closer to the elegant home. He needed a minute to adjust the plan anyway.

Absently he hummed along with Johnnie Taylor singing "Everything's Out in the Open." Finally, he decided there was no way he could get it done out here, maybe not today at all. He'd enjoyed the adventure, though. A sudden shaft of light illuminated the cab of his car, just about stopping his heart. Behind him was one of those gigantic F-250 redneck specials with the roof lights. As it crept around him, his paused heart went into overdrive, and his stomach bubbled. Without incident, the monster truck drove into the circular driveway behind the Bug. Jimmy knew this couldn't be good. His instinct was on point because not two minutes later, the Winfrey boy came racing out of that ornate door, naked as the day he was born. Jimmy and the Plymouth burned rubber out of there.

RAPE SUSPECT SHOT IN RENA LARA
HOME INVASION

December 4, 2000

Chickamauga County Sheriff officials report an eighteen-year-old man has succumbed to the injuries sustained in a Rena Lara home invasion rape/robbery attempt. The suspect, identified as Emanuel J. Winfrey, is the son of prominent area minister and businessman Sabre Winfrey. Winfrey was a standout scholar and athlete with no prior criminal record.

On Monday afternoon, Jimmy sat on his living room sofa with the news and Caticia's soft, small hand in his own. Her nails were bitten-down, and she smelled like twelve types of fruit. He was surprised she nor Asia had asthma from all that spraying and glossing they did. He started to chuckle, but oddly enough, after everything that had gone down, he was conflicted; he pulled his daughter closer.

"How you feelin', Punkin?"

He could feel her shrug. Several quiet moments passed, and then she cleared her throat.

"I just want to forget," she said.

"That'll probably be the best thing," he said, and then: "I wonder if it will be open casket."

~~~~~

Even though Jimmy told his daughter to forget, he could not. Two weeks later, he drove to the fune just to see if it was all real. He approached the fortresslike building head-on. Its grand columns were wrapped in garland and infinite crimson lengths of velvet in honor of the Christmas season. Two huge wreaths dangled from its elegant glass doors. Seemed to Jimmy that the sun shone directly on the cross that extended from the roof; yet, it provided little insurance against the thirty-five-degree temperatures. Jimmy exited his car and pulled his leather jacket over his uniform and zipped it. He figured they would put the boy away nice, but he saw so many limos on the way, the gathering could have been easily mistaken for some kind of red-carpet event. He slipped through the processional of family members readying to enter the church; neither the Reverend nor the First Lady was in the mix. There was a group of light-brights near the front that must be the First Lady's people, he thought. Inside the church were soft organ music and enough niggas for a Tarzan movie; he wedged himself in the very last seat on the very last pew.

Between the bodies and the heat cranked up, he was already too warm.

"I can't believe his fine ass dead," said the teenaged girl beside him. "He didn't have to rape nobody, let alone a white girl."

"Quit cussing in the house of the Lord," her friend said.

"My bad," the girl said, and popped her gum.

She was fanning herself with the huge, glossy obituary. The Winfrey boy's face went back and forth and back and forth, and every time his eyes seemed to catch Jimmy's. He tore his gaze away, glanced up, and saw the First Lady, held together by two tall men who looked identical, but she didn't get two feet into the room before she was fainting, falling, carried away.

EPILOGUE

PRISCILLA

EMANUEL J. WINFREY
SEPTEMBER 10, 1982–DECEMBER 4, 2000

Emanuel John Winfrey was born September 10, 1982, to Reverend and Mrs. Sabre Winfrey and a boisterous band of four brothers. Fearfully and wonderfully made, Emanuel grew up under the watchful eye of the community that loved and nurtured him. He was united with the body of Christ through baptism at an early age and loved the Lord through action and deed. He was a member of the Seven Seals Missionary Baptist Church, where he sang in the youth choir and served as a house musician, junior Sunday school teacher, and president of the Boys to Men club. A gifted musician, he played the piano, drums, bass, and basically whatever was handed to him.

Emanuel excelled secularly as well. An award-winning athlete and scholar, he was a member of the Superintendent's Academy, the Mu Alpha Theta math honor society, the Dominion Academy jazz band, and the Masters of Learning Honor Society. He volunteered with the Special Olympics and the Chickamauga Cares Program. He holds state records for passing and rushing yards as a quarterback, medaled in the Junior Olympics in the high jump, and was chosen for the *Clarion Ledger*'s Dandy Dozen more times than any other football player in the state. Before his life was tragically cut short, Emanuel was choosing between full-ride scholarships from Vanderbilt, Florida State, and Louisiana State Universities.

Emanuel was loved by many. Left to cherish his memory: his mother, Priscilla Stringer Winfrey; his father, Rev. Sabre J. Winfrey; his brothers Sabre III, Moshe, Mack, and Ivy Winfrey; as well as a host of family and friends. He was preceded in his death by his grandparents, Sabre and Etta Winfrey and Taliaferro and Cassandra Curry Stringer, his uncles Mack and Merwin Winfrey, and a special aunt, Annie Stringer Williams.

DIAMOND

We used to play this game in school called "Telephone," where the teacher would whisper a message in the first kid's ear, and that kid shared the message with the next, who shared it with the next and so on down the line until it reached the last person in the room, who then reported the result to class. My favorite part was seeing how drastically the message changed as it traveled from ear to ear. According to the teacher, that was the worst part, and it took growing up to realize why. Information changed in the mouth of each teller, and despite whether it occurred intentionally or was simply lost in translation, the truth was damaged each time it was told. And when the message was less than the truth in the first place, well, the theories become speculation, and the lies become more blatant.

My life felt like that game since damn near every ear and mouth in the city were in on the conversation about the death of Rev. Winfrey's son. Most were just trying to see if the Rev was gone get Jesse Jackson or Al Sharpton them to come march until the DA decided to prosecute the girl's daddy for shooting Wonderboy in the back. The DA flat out refused to do so, being the girl's daddy's friend and all, seeing that the Winfrey boy was in the middle of the commission of a heinous crime (which his mama and daddy have consistently denied). The *Press Register* wouldn't even let the Winfreys run the funeral notice in their pages. Folk said that the editor, Floyd Ingram, who had once been one of the Reverend's staunchest allies, had said that disgusting thug wasn't worth being eulogized in his paper.

Despite everything I heard and knew, despite the fact I had set his death in motion myself, there was no preparation for seeing Wonder unmoving in that casket. But between the good-ass weed Yancey's friend had got me and one of the First Lady's nerve pills, I was floating and falling at the same time. He wore a pinstriped navy suit with a matching vest, a navy tie, and a light blue shirt. I think it was the suit he took his senior portraits in, but he had gained heft since then, muscle, so I couldn't for sure tell. The body there was not the same as the one that had once blanketed mine.

Emanuel Winfrey. Wonderboy. Wonder. Which one of those might have killed my brother? Or hurt those girls? Which one had said he'd love me forever and then lost interest in all we had? For all the things I didn't and couldn't know, I no longer wanted to carry his baby. I couldn't tell for sure I would know how to love it with all I knew. People were saying Wonderboy had to be the last casualty of the Reaping Season, but I knew that not to be true. The last will be his baby, and only Mrs. Kathareen and I will know why and how. My belly cramped through the entire funeral service. Although it would be yet more of the loss that I recognized so well, I knew it was necessary to lose them both to be free. Free to learn who I am. Free to go to college. Free to find my siblings. Free to discover love for real one day. And that began when I saw his casket hanging above that deep, final hole and understood that it would never rise again.

In the Joker's notebook, he called himself a grief taker, a salt-eater, and at first, I thought that was his regular bit of nonsense, but I realize he was talking about people like me. And towns like Dominion. And states like Mississippi, where there had been sadness heaped on sorrow heaped on pain. But unlike the Joker or Dominion or Mississippi, it wouldn't be my forever. I would be leaving, and I wouldn't be taking the bullshit along with me.

ACKNOWLEDGMENTS

Victoria, my sister, friend, diviner, and first story reader, thank you for always believing in me. I love you.

Ma, thank you for giving me books with no leash, your unending support, and your belief in my talent. I love you and Roy.

Anthony, your love and support anchor me and helped make this time possible.

To my namesake, Big Addie, I love you to life. Thank you for Toni and Floyd and always being willing to give me whatever my whim decided. You are my sweetness in this world. Aunts Annie, Gale, Terrie, and Carla—thank you, wonderful women, for being part of the seven sisters who made me who I am. Thank you, my lovely, Kourtni Luster—I kinda owe you my life.

My dear friend Kandelorea, you match my warrior; we in this thing together like booty hair. I will always go hard for you, as you do me. My brother, Lamar, thank you for your listening ear.

To the thousand mothers of my Black girlhood, like Mrs. Margaret McGlown, Mrs. Shirley Catchings, Mrs. Daisy Burnett, Ms. Wanda Lee, Ms. Olenza McBride, as well as those who have departed this realm, like Mrs. Estella Yarbrough, Mrs. Annie Williams, Ms. Casandra Curry, yall were among the first to declare me talented and call on me to perform. Thank you for allowing me to express myself before the world told me I wasn't enough.

ACKNOWLEDGMENTS

To my eighth-grade home ec teacher, Mrs. Chow, I told you I was going to put you in my novel when you gave me detention for talking in your class, and now I am finally able to do it. Principal Jeff King, RIP—thank you for letting me know I could do anything.

Maurice Ruffin, you my dog!! Kiese Laymon, Jamey Hatley, my fellow Memphissippi Mafia, we locked in for life, or else! I love yall. Thank you. Thank you. Thank you. Also, Annell López, thank you, doll!

PJ Mark, thank you for your darling, enthusiastic, smart, dapper self. You know what you're doing.

Jenna, you were this book's midwife. *Dominion* would not have been what it is without your wisdom. Farrar, Straus and Giroux, the fellowship changed my life. Thanks for seeing me.

Finally, I want to thank myself for cultivating the courage, imagination, and curiosity to create worlds. You did that, Addie.

A NOTE ABOUT THE AUTHOR

Addie E. Citchens was born in Clarksdale, Mississippi, and lives in New Orleans. A graduate of Jackson State University, she studied in the Florida State University Creative Writing Program and the Callaloo Creative Writing Workshop. Her work has appeared in *The New Yorker*, *The Paris Review*, the *Oxford American*'s "Best of the South," Midnight & Indigo's speculative fiction anthology, and other publications. Her blues history work features prominently in *Mississippi Folklife*, and she has been heard on *The Mississippi Arts Hour* on Mississippi Public Broadcasting. She was the inaugural recipient of the Farrar, Straus and Giroux Writer's Fellowship, and her short story "That Girl" won the O. Henry Prize. *Dominion* is her first novel.